"Then tell me i~
took hold of he~

"Very well." Callie indignantly tried to snatch her hand but Lukas held on. "I do not have a lover, Lukas."

"A boyfriend then? A partner of some description?"

"No, none of those things. Now kindly let me go."

"What then? Tell me. Because I can see it, Calista. I can see it in your eyes."

Callie hesitated. She could feel the moment closing in on her, weighing down on her with leaden pressure. Suddenly there was no escape.

"I do not have a lover, Lukas." She summoned the words from deep inside her, where the truth had lain dormant for so long. "But I do have a child."

"A child?" He dropped her arm as if it were made of molten metal. "You have a child?"

"Yes." She watched as the shock that had contorted his handsome features settled into a brutal grimace of stone. "I have a four-and-a-half-year-old daughter."

She paused, sucking in a breath as if it might be her last. *This was it.*

"And so, Lukas, do you."

Secret Heirs of Billionaires

There are some things money can't buy...

Living life at lightning pace, these magnates
are no strangers to stakes at their highest.
It seems they've got it all... That is until they
find out that there's an unplanned item to
add to their list of accomplishments!

Achieved:

1. Successful business empire

2. Beautiful women in their bed

3. *An heir to bear their name?*

Though every billionaire needs to leave his
legacy in safe hands, discovering a secret
heir shakes up his carefully orchestrated plan
in more ways than one!

Uncover their secrets in:

Unwrapping the Castelli Secret by Caitlin Crews

Brunetti's Secret Son by Maya Blake

The Secret to Marrying Marchesi by Amanda Cinelli

Demetriou Demands His Child by Kate Hewitt

The Desert King's Secret Heir by Annie West

The Sheikh's Secret Son by Maggie Cox

The Innocent's Shameful Secret by Sara Craven

Look out for more stories in the **Secret Heirs
of Billionaires** series coming soon!

Andie Brock

THE GREEK'S
PLEASURABLE REVENGE

HARLEQUIN PRESENTS®

Recycling programs
for this product may
not exist in your area.

ISBN-13: 978-0-373-06076-4

The Greek's Pleasurable Revenge

First North American Publication 2017

Copyright © 2017 by Andrea Brock

Printed in U.S.A.

Andie Brock started inventing imaginary friends around the age of four and is still doing that today—only now the sparkly fairies have made way for spirited heroines and sexy heroes. Thankfully, she now has some real friends, as well as a husband and three children, plus a grumpy but lovable cat. Andie lives in Bristol and when not actually writing might well be plotting her next passionate romance story.

Books by Andie Brock

Harlequin Presents

The Last Heir of Monterrato

Wedlocked!
Bound by His Desert Diamond

One Night With Consequences
The Shock Cassano Baby

Society Weddings
The Sheikh's Wedding Contract

Visit the Author Profile page at Harlequin.com for more titles.

This one is for Bill. Don't worry, you don't have to read it! Love, M xx

CHAPTER ONE

'WE DON'T WANT any trouble, Kalanos.'

Lukas roughly shook off the hand on the sleeve of his dark suit, before turning to give its owner a bone-chilling stare.

'Trouble?' He let his eyes travel slowly over the sweating face of the middle-aged man who was trying but failing miserably to square up to him. 'Whatever makes you think I would bring any *trouble*, Yiannis?'

The man took a step away, glancing around for back-up. 'Look, Kalanos, this is my father's funeral—that's all I'm saying. It's a time for respect.'

'Ah, yes, *respect*.' Lukas let the word slide through his teeth like a witch's curse. 'I'm so glad you reminded me. That must be why there are so many people here.' He swept a derisive stare over the sparsely populated graveside. 'So many people wanting to pay their "re-spects" to the great man.'

'It's a quiet family funeral. That's all.' Yiannis avoided his eye. 'And you are not wanted here, Lukas.'

'No?' Lukas ground out his reply. 'Well, you know what? That's too bad.'

In point of fact Lukas hadn't wanted to be there. Not yet. Lukas had been far from ready to bury this evil man. He'd had plans for him. The man who had killed his father as surely as if he had driven a blade through his heart. Whose evil machinations had seen Lukas thrown into prison for a crime he hadn't committed. Dark, unspeakable plans that would have seen him begging for mercy and, on realising there was none to be had, pleading for the oblivion of death.

Four and a half years. That was how long Lukas had been incarcerated in one of Athens's toughest jails, with only the dregs of society for company. Plenty of time to go over every detail of his betrayal, and worse—far worse—the betrayal of his father. Years of seething, boiling, melting rage that had solidified inside him until it had become all he was. No longer a man of flesh and blood but hard and cold, hewn from the lava of hatred.

Four and a half years to plot his revenge.

And all for nothing.

Because the object of his hatred, Aristotle Gianopoulous, had died on the very same day that Lukas had been released from prison. Almost as if he had timed it deliberately. Almost as if he had known.

Now Lukas watched the coffin being slowly lowered into the ground as the sonorous voice of the priest bestowing his final blessing filled the air. His cold eyes travelled round the circle of black-clad mourners, moving from one to the next. He let his gaze stay just long enough for his forbidding presence to register, to unsettle them, to shift their focus from the dead man to one who was very much alive. And who wanted them to know it.

Beside him Yiannis Gianopoulous fidgeted nervously, shooting him wary sidelong glances. The son of Aristotle from his second marriage, he was of no interest to Lukas. His brother Christos was here too, scowling at him from the relative safety of the other side of the open grave. There were a couple of old business associates, Aristotle's ancient lawyer, and one of his lady-friends, quietly dabbing at her eyes as if it was expected of her. Slightly to one side stood Petros and Dorcas, Aristotle's last remaining faithful employees, who had worked for him for longer than Lukas could remember. More fool them.

An assorted array of damaged and broken individuals, the detritus of Gianopoulous's life, all brought together under the punishing heat of the midday sun on this beautiful Greek island to bury the man who had doubtless managed to blight all their lives in one way or another. Lukas didn't give a damn about any of them.

All except for one.

Finally he let his eyes rest upon her. The slightly built young woman standing with her head bowed, clutching a single white lily tightly in her hand. Calista Gianopoulous. *Callie.* The offspring of Aristotle's third wife, his youngest child and only daughter. The one good thing Aristotle had produced. Or so Lukas had thought. Until she had betrayed him, too. Playing her part in his downfall in the most treacherous way possible.

Lukas allowed himself a moment to savour her discomfort. He had recognised her immediately, of course, the second he had burst onto this touching scene. Marching through the small graveyard, past the neglected resting place of his own father, he had stormed towards the freshly dug grave, enjoying the palpable wave of alarm that had rippled across the mourners.

And the look of panic that had gripped Calista. He had seen it, even though she was wearing a veil, had witnessed the flash of terror in those green eyes, registered the way her slender body swayed slightly before she had steadied herself and looked down.

Now he watched as she bowed her head still further, pulling at the black lace that covered her glorious red hair as if she could somehow disguise herself, hide from him. But there was no chance of that. No chance at all.

Look at me, Calista.

He found himself willing her to raise her eyes, to meet his searing gaze. He wanted to see her guilt for himself, to witness her shame, to feel it penetrate the solid wall of his contempt.

Or was some small, pathetic part of him still hoping that he'd got it wrong?

But Calista's eyes were firmly fixed on the grave before her, looking for all the world as if she would jump in with her deceased father if it meant she could get away from him. But, no. She would have no such escape. Aristotle might have died before Lukas could exact his revenge, but Calista was here before him—ready for the taking. It would be revenge of a very different kind, but none the less pleasurable for that.

Lukas stared at her through narrowed eyes. The young woman he thought he'd known. How wrong he had been. Over the years they had built up a friendship, or so he had thought, sharing their summers on the island of Thalassa, a private idyll bought jointly by their two fathers when G&K Shipping had made its first million. A symbol of their success and their enduring friendship.

So much for that.

Lukas, eight years Calista's senior, thought back to the lonely little kid whose parents had divorced before she'd barely been out of nappies. Her neurotic screwball of a mother had whisked her back to her homeland of England, but sent her alone to Thalassa for the school holidays. Cutting a forlorn figure, Calista had trailed after whichever half-sibling had happened to be in residence at the sumptuous Gianopoulous residence at the time, her fair skin turning pink in the hot Greek sun, freckles dotting her nose.

She had trailed after Lukas too, seeking him out on his family's side of the island, obstinately settling herself in his boat when he was off one of his fishing trips, or clambering over the rocks to watch him dive into the crystal-clear turquoise waters before pestering him to show her how it was done.

Later she had become Callie the awkward teenager. Motherless by then, she'd been packed off to boarding school, but had still came back to Thalassa for the long summer vacations. Hiding her mop of curly red hair beneath a floppy straw hat and her pretty face behind the fat pages of a blockbuster novel, she'd no longer had any interest in her brothers—nor, seemingly, in Lukas, except for the occasional giveaway glance from those amazing green eyes when she'd thought he wasn't looking, and blushing to the roots of her hair when he caught her out.

Callie, now Calista, who at eighteen, had somehow metamorphosed into the most stunning young woman. *And had tempted him into bed.* Although technically they had never actually made it as far as a bed. Caught up in the moment, the sofa in the living room had served them well enough.

Lukas had known it was wrong at the time—of course he had. But she had been just too alluring, too enticing to resist. He had been surprised, flattered— honoured, even—that she had made a play for him, chosen him to take her virginity. But most of all he had been duped.

And now he was going to make her pay.

Calista felt the ground sway beneath her feet, and the image of the coffin bearing her father blurred through the black lace of her veil.

Oh, please, no.

Not Lukas—not here, not now. But there was no mistaking the figure of the man who was glowering at her from the other side of the grave, or the power of his intensely dark stare as it bored into her. He was broader than she remembered him, and his muscled torso harder, stronger, more imposing, filling the well-cut dark suit like steel poured into a mould of the finest fabric. His sleeves tugged tight against the bulge of his biceps as he stood there with his arms folded across his chest, his feet firmly planted, clearly indicating that he was going nowhere.

All this Calista registered in a flash of panic before lowering her eyes to the grave.

This couldn't be happening.

Lukas Kalanos was in prison—everybody knew that. Serving a long sentence for his part in the disgraceful arms smuggling business that had been masterminded by his father, Stavros—her own father's business partner.

The sheer immorality of the venture had sickened Calista to the core—it still did. The fact that her father's shipping business had gone bust because of it, and her family had been financially ruined, was only of secondary concern. At the age of twenty-three she had already experienced great wealth and great hardship. And she knew which one she preferred.

Which was why five years ago she had walked away, determined to turn her back on her tainted Greek heritage. Away from the collapse of the multi-billion-dollar family business, from her brothers' bickering and back-stabbing. From her father's towering rages and black, alcohol-fuelled depressions.

But most of all she had walked away from Lukas Kalanos—the man whose dark eyes were tearing into her soul right now. The man who had taken her virginity and broken her heart. And who had left her with a very permanent reminder.

At the thought of her little daughter Calista felt her lip start to quiver. Effie was fine—she was safe at home in London, probably running rings around poor Magda, Calista's trusted friend and fellow student nurse, who was in charge until Calista could hurry back. She didn't want to spend any more time here than she had to—she was intending to stay a couple of days at most, to sort through her father's things with her brothers, sign whatever paperwork needed to be signed and then escape from this island for ever.

But suddenly getting away from Thalassa had taken on a new urgency. And getting away from the menacingly dark form of Lukas Kalanos more imperative still.

The burial ceremony was almost over. The priest was inviting them to join him in the last prayer before the mourners tossed flowers and soil onto the top of the coffin, the distinctive sound as they met the polished wood sending a shiver through Calista's slender frame.

'Not cold, surely?' A firm, possessive grip clasped her elbow. 'Or is this a touching display of grief?'

He spoke in faultless English, although Calista's Greek would have been more than good enough to understand his meaning. Using his grasp, he turned her so that now she couldn't escape the full force of him as he loomed over her, glowered down at her. 'If so, I'm sure I don't need to point out that it is seriously misplaced.'

'Lukas, please…' Calista braced herself to meet his searing gaze, her knees almost giving way at the sight of him.

The tangled dark curls had gone, in favour of a close-cropped style that hardened his handsome features, accentuating the uncompromising sweep of his jawline shadowed with designer stubble, the sharp-angled planes of his cheeks. But the eyes were the same—so dark a brown as to be almost black, breath-taking in their intensity.

'I am here to bury my father—not listen to your insults.'

'Oh, believe me, *agapi mou*, in terms of insults I wouldn't know where to start. It would take a lifetime and more to even scratch the surface of the depths of my revulsion for that man.'

Calista swallowed hard. Her father had had his faults—she had no doubt about that. A larger-than-life character, both in temperament and girth, he had treated her mother very badly, and had had a series of affairs that had broken her mother's spirit, albeit al-ready fragile. In turn that had eventually led to her accidental overdose. Calista would never wholly for-give him for that.

But he'd still been her father—the only one she would ever have—and she had always known she would have to return to Thalassa one last time to lay him to rest. And maybe lay some of her demons to rest too.

Little had she known that the biggest demon of all would be present at the graveside, sliding his arm around her waist right now in a blatant show of pos-sessiveness and control.

'I'll thank you not to speak of my father in that way.'

She was grateful to feel her hot-headed temper kick-ing in to rescue her, colouring her cheeks beneath the veil. Pointedly taking a step to the side to dislodge his hand from her elbow, she pushed back her shoulders and had to stifle a gasp as his arm slid around her waist, the ring of muscled steel burning through the thin fabric of her black dress.

'It is both disrespectful and deeply insulting.' Her voice shook alarmingly. 'Quite aside from which, *you* are hardly in a position to judge anyone.'

'Me, Calista?' Dark brows were raised fractionally in feigned surprise. 'Why would that be?'

'You know perfectly well why.'

'Ah, yes. The heinous crime I committed. That's something I want to talk to you about.'

'Well, I don't want to talk to *you*—about that or anything else.'

Particularly not anything else.

Cold fingers of dread tiptoed down her spine at the thought of what they might end up discussing. If Lukas were to find out that he had a daughter, heaven only knew how he would react. It was too terrifying an idea to contemplate.

Calista had never intended to keep Effie a secret from her father—at least not at first. She had been over five months pregnant before she had even realised it herself, convinced that stress was responsible for the nausea, her lack of periods, her fatigue. Because *no one* got pregnant the very first time they had sex, did they?

Certainly the stress she had been suffering would have felled the strongest spirit, even *before* she'd found out she was expecting Lukas's child. What with Stavros—her father's friend and business partner—

dying so suddenly, and then the whole arms smuggling scandal coming out and the shipping business collapsing. And finally making the sickening discovery that Lukas was involved.

By the time she had seen a doctor Lukas had already been awaiting trial for his crime. And on the day she'd gone into labour, a full month earlier than expected, alone and frightened as she pushed her way through the agonising birth with only the midwife's hand to grip for support, Lukas had been in court, with the judge declaring him guilty and sentencing him to eight years in jail.

Effie's first screaming lungful of air had come at the exact moment when the judge had uttered the fateful words, 'Take him down.'

On that day—the day of her daughter's birth—Calista had resolved to wait to tell Lukas of Effie's existence until he was released from jail. Eight years had seemed a lifetime away. Time enough for her and Effie to build their own lives in the UK, to become a strong, independent unit. So the secret had been kept well hidden.

Calista had told no one—not even her father—for fear that if he knew the truth word would spread amongst her Greek family and find its way to Lukas. But if she was honest there was another reason she didn't want her father to know. She didn't want her precious Effie tainted by any association with him.

He would have tried to take control, Calista knew that—both of her and his granddaughter. He would have tried to manipulate them, bend them to his will, use them to his advantage. Calista had worked far too hard to build an independent life to let him do that. Simply not telling him about Effie had been the easiest solution all round.

Now Aristotle would never know he'd had a granddaughter. But Lukas… Calista moved inside the band of his arm, her heart thudding with frantic alarm and something else—something that felt dangerously like excitement. Lukas would have to know that he was a father. That was his right. But not yet. Not until Calista had had a chance to prepare herself—and Effie. Not until she had made sure all her defences were securely in place.

'Calista, people are leaving.' Beside her, but keeping a safe distance from Lukas, Yiannis tried to get her attention. 'They are waiting to speak to us before they go.'

'Leaving so soon?' Lukas gave a derisive sneer. 'Is there to be no wake? No toasting the life of the great man?'

'The boats are waiting to take everyone back to the mainland.' Yiannis wiped the sweat from his brow. 'You'll be on one of them, if you know what's good for you.'

Lukas gave a gruff laugh. 'Funny, I was just thinking the same thing about you.'

'You have brought ruination and disgrace to our family, Kalanos, but Thalassa is the one asset my father managed to protect. You may own half of it now, but not for much longer.'

'Is that right?'

'Yes. We intend to make a claim for your half of the island as compensation for the financial ruin you and your father caused us. Our lawyers are confident we will win the case.' Yiannis struggled to keep his voice firm.

'We?'

'My brother and I. And Calista, of course.'

At the mention of her name Lukas released his arm from her waist, turning to give Calista a stare of such revulsion that it churned her stomach. She had no idea what Yiannis was talking about. She had never agreed to instruct a lawyer to sue for compensation. She wanted nothing to do with Thalassa—even the small share she assumed she'd inherit now, on Aristotle's death. She certainly had no intention of fighting Lukas for his half.

'Well, good luck with that.' Narrowing his eyes, Lukas turned away, seemingly bored with the subject. 'Actually, no.' Turning back, he fixed Yiannis with a punishing stare. 'You might as well know—both of you. The island of Thalassa now belongs to me. *All* of it.'

'Yeah, right.' Christos had joined them, positioning himself between Yiannis and Lukas, sweating profusely. 'Do you take us for idiots, Kalanos?'

Lukas's pursed lips gave an almost imperceptible twitch.

'You are obviously lying.'

'I'm afraid not.' Lukas removed a tiny speck of dust from the sleeve of his immaculate suit. 'I'm only surprised your lawyers didn't tell you. I managed to acquire your father's half of the island some time ago.'

Christos's face turned puce, but it was Yiannis who spoke. 'That can't be true. Aristotle would never have sold to you.'

'He didn't need to. When he and my father bought the island they registered it in their wives' names. A touching gesture, don't you think? Or am I being naive? Perhaps it was simply a tax dodge? Either way, it has proved very convenient. *My* half, of course, came to me upon the death of my mother—God rest her soul. Acquiring *your* half was simply a matter of tracking down Aristotle's first wife and making her an offer she couldn't refuse. I can't tell you how grateful she was. Especially as she had no idea she owned it.'

'But you have been in prison for years. How could you possibly have done this?'

'You'd be surprised. It turns out that you can make some very useful contacts inside. Very useful indeed.' Lukas raised a dark brow. 'I now know just the man for any given job. And I do mean *any.*'

Yiannis visibly paled beneath his swarthy skin. In desperation he turned to Calista, but she only gave a small shrug. She didn't give a damn who owned the island. She just wanted to get off it as fast as she could.

Christos, meanwhile, always blessed with more brawn than brains, had raised his fists in a pathetic show of aggression. 'You don't scare me, Kalanos. I'll take you on any time you like.'

'Didn't I hear you say you had a boat to catch?' With a display of supreme indifference Lukas treated him to an icily withering look.

Christos took a step forward, but Yiannis grabbed hold of his arm, pulling him away to stop him from getting himself into real trouble. As he twisted sideways his feet got caught in the green tarpaulin covering the fresh earth around the grave and they both stumbled, lurching dangerously towards the grave itself, before righting themselves at the last moment.

Yiannis tugged at his brother's arm again, desperate to get him away from humiliation, or a punch on the nose, or both.

'You haven't heard the last of this, Kalanos!' Christos shouted over his shoulder as his brother hastily manoeuvred them away, weaving between the overgrown graves. 'You are going to pay for this.'

Calista watched in surprise as her half-brothers disappeared. Weren't they supposed to have been staying a couple of nights on the island to go through their father's papers and sort out his affairs? Clearly that was no longer happening. Neither did they seem bothered about leaving her behind to deal with Lukas. It was obviously every man for himself— or *her*self.

But it did mean that there was nothing to keep her there any more. Unless she counted the formidably dark figure that was still rooted ominously by her side.

Realising she was still clutching the single lily in her hand, she stepped towards the grave and let it drop, whispering a silent goodbye to her father. A lump lodged in her throat. Not just for her father—her relationship with him had always been too fraught, too blighted by anguish and tragedy for simple grief to sum it up—but because Calista knew she was not just saying goodbye to Aristotle but to Thalassa, her childhood, her Greek heritage. This was the end of an era.

She turned to go, immediately coming up against the solid wall of Lukas's chest. Adjusting the strap of her bag over her shoulder, she went to move past him. 'If you will excuse me I need to be going.'

'Going where, exactly?'

'I'm leaving the island with the others, of course. There is no point in me staying here any longer.'

'Oh, but there is.' With lightning speed Lukas closed his hand around her wrist, bringing her back up against his broad chest. 'You, *agape*, are going nowhere.'

Calista flinched, her whole body going into a kind of panicky meltdown that sent a flood of fear rippling down to her core. Bizarrely, it wasn't an entirely unpleasant sensation.

'What do you mean by that?'

'Just what I say. You and I have unfinished business. And you won't be leaving Thalassa until I say so.'

'So what do you intend to do? Hold me prisoner?'

'If necessary, yes.'

'Don't be ridiculous.'

She hardened her voice as best she could, determined that she would stand up to this new, frighteningly formidable Lukas. Pulling away, she looked pointedly at her wrist until he released it.

'Anyway, what *is* this unfinished business? As far as I'm concerned we have nothing to discuss.'

Her nails dug into her palms at the blatant lie. But he couldn't be talking about Effie. If he had found out about his daughter he would have blown her whole world apart by now.

'Don't tell me you have forgotten, Calista. Because I certainly haven't.'

Dark, dark eyes looked down on her, glittering with intent.

'Let's just say the image of you lying semi-naked on my sofa, your legs wrapped around my back, has stayed with me all these years. I've probably conjured it up more times than I should have. Prison has that effect on you. You have to take your pleasures where you can.'

Callie blushed to the roots of her hair, grateful for the black veil that still partially obscured her mortified face. That was until Lukas gently, almost reverentially, lifted the fine lace and arranged it back over her head. For one bizarre moment she thought he was going to kiss her, as if she were some sort of dark bride.

'There—that's better.'

He stared at her, drinking her in like a man with the fiercest thirst. She held her breath. Each testosterone-fuelled second seemed longer than the last. She shifted beneath his astonishingly powerful scrutiny, her skin prickling, her heart pounding in her ribcage.

'I had forgotten how beautiful you are, Calista.'

Her stifled breath came out as a gasp. She hadn't expected a compliment—not after all the bullying and the veiled threats. Except this was a compliment deliberately tinged with menace.

'I can't tell you how much I am looking forward to renewing our acquaintance. I've been looking forward to it for almost five long years.'

No! Calista choked back a silent cry.

Surely he didn't think she would repeat that catastrophic error? Panic and outrage stiffened her spine.

'If you imagine that I am going to go to bed with you again, Lukas, you are sorely mistaken.'

'Bed…sofa…up against the wall right here in front of your father's grave, if you like. It's all the same to me. I want you, Calista. And I should warn you, when I want something I go all out to make sure that I get it.'

CHAPTER TWO

LUKAS WATCHED THE alarm on Calista's face set her delicate features in stone.

He had been right to declare her beautiful—even if he *had* only meant to say it in his head. She was even more beautiful than he remembered. The intervening years had honed her heart-shaped face, the high cheekbones, the firmly pointed chin. But the small, straight nose was still speckled with a dusting of freckles and her mouth… That was just as he remembered it, wide and full-lipped and deliciously pink—even now, when it was pursed in an attempt at defiance.

How Aristotle had produced such an exquisite creature as this was almost beyond comprehension. Calista obviously took after her mother, Diana, the actress-cum-model whose beauty had ultimately been her downfall. They certainly shared the same colouring, but whereas Diana had been all leggy height and stunning bone structure, which the camera had loved, Calista was petite, with full breasts and a slim waist leading to curvaceous hips that begged to be traced with the flat of his palm. Lukas could feel that urge powering through him right now, and he responded by reaching for her hand, relishing the soft feel of it beneath his own.

'This way.' He started off across the graveyard, pulling Calista behind him, all too aware that he was behaving like some sort of caveman but not caring in the least.

'Lukas—stop this.'

No way. Her feeble protestation only made him all the more determined that she was going to come with him—back to his villa and back to his bed. He had waited far too long for this moment to allow any second thoughts to creep in, or even to let common decency stand in his way. Certainly not her breathless objections.

'Lukas, stop—let me go!'

They had reached the small copse behind the ancient chapel, where he had left his motorbike. Positioning Calista between it and him, Lukas finally let go of her hand.

Calista snatched it back, her eyes flashing with fire. 'Just what the hell do you think you are playing at?'

'Oh, I'm not playing, Calista. This is no game.'

'What, then? What are you trying to prove? Why are you behaving like such a…a horrible bully?'

'Perhaps that's what I've become.' He gave her a casually brutal stare. 'Perhaps that's what four and a half years in prison does to a man.'

Calista's expression tightened. 'I don't even understand why you aren't still there. You were sentenced to *eight* years.'

'Time off for good behaviour.' His eyes glittered coldly. 'You see, I was a very good boy whilst I was in there—as far as the authorities were concerned, that is. Now I intend to make up for it.'

He watched her swallow.

'I do hope my early release hasn't inconvenienced you?'

'It hasn't. I couldn't care less where you are…what you do.'

'Good. Then get on the bike. We are going to Villa Helene.'

'No, we are *not*.' Her hand flew to her chest. 'I'm not going anywhere with you.'

'And there I was, hoping we wouldn't have to do this the hard way.'

Easily spanning her waist with his broad hands, Lukas lifted her off her feet and planted her unceremoniously on the pillion seat of the bike. The thin fabric of her skirt rode up over her thighs, pulling seductively taut, while her breasts heaved with indignation.

Lukas fought down the kick of lust.

'If you don't get me off this thing right now I am going to scream.'

'Feel free.' He smiled darkly. 'It won't make any difference. Your dear brothers, along with the other broken-hearted mourners, are already on their way back to the mainland. No one will hear you.'

He saw the flicker of fear in her eyes but she didn't move. Her pride refused to give him the satisfaction. And for some reason that only increased his admiration—and his arousal. Perched on the leather seat of his bike, she looked like some sort of erotic goddess, her back arched in defiance, her glorious Titian hair tumbling over her shoulders. The mourning veil, he noticed, had fallen to the dry ground at his feet.

'There's Petros…and Dorcas. They're still on the island. Villa Melina is still their home.'

He gave her a telling look. That was something for *him* to decide—not her. Clearly she was forgetting who called the shots around here.

'Look…' She suddenly changed tack, trying for a conciliatory tone. 'What's this all about, anyway?'

'You used to love this bike, Callie, don't you remember?' He deliberately used her shortened name, taking them back to the long hot summers of their shared past. 'You were forever pestering me for a ride.'

They had both loved this motorbike—the sleek black beast that had been Lukas's sixteenth birthday present to himself. He'd had other bikes since, and sports cars, luxury yachts, a helicopter—all the extravagant modes of transport that great wealth could afford. But nothing had surpassed the feeling of straddling this powerful beauty all those years ago, made even better by the feel of Callie's skinny arms clinging to his waist as they had roared off, the sound of her excited squeals in his ear.

Coming across it in the garage this morning, just where he had left it, he had felt as if he were meeting an old friend. One old friend, at least, that hadn't let him down. She had obediently started first time after he had charged the battery.

'I think we've both grown up since then.' Calista

tossed back her flame-red hair, all sharp-angled defiance and dignified posturing. 'Or at least *I* have.'

'Indeed… I wouldn't dispute that.' Lukas gave a derisive laugh. 'I seem to remember we engaged in some *very* grown-up activity last time we met.'

Again she flushed, as if she found the memory of what they had done intensely shameful. As well she might.

'Well, that's not something that is going to be repeated, I can assure you. Despite your earlier threats.'

'Not threats, Calista. Think of it more as a promise.'

'You are such an arrogant piece of work, Lukas, you know that?' Emerald eyes flashed with fire. 'I promise you this: what happened between us will *never* happen again.'

'No? You're sure about that, are you?'

'Quite sure.'

'Then coming back to my villa for a couple of hours won't hurt, will it? Unless you don't trust yourself, of course?'

'I trust myself, Lukas. It's *you* I don't trust.'

'Ah, yes, of course. I keep forgetting that *I'm* the villain of the piece here.'

'Yes, you are!' Calista immediately fired back at him.

He had to hand it to her—her acting skills had improved significantly over the years.

'In that case let me reassure you that nothing will happen between us unless you want it to.'

Was that true? It should be. His well-rehearsed plan had always been to trick her into wanting him, just the way she had him. But if she carried on looking at him the way she was now he wasn't sure he'd be able to hang on to his control.

He studied her from beneath lowered lashes, lazily, slowing himself down. Unless he was very much mistaken there was something else in that fiery look of hers. For all her prim deportment, her expression of outrage, her feisty comebacks, *something* simmered beneath the surface. Something that looked remarkably like sexual arousal. *Yes.* He would have her screaming his name with pleasure before the day was through. And then revenge would be his.

Swinging his leg over the bike, he turned the key in the ignition, gripping the handlebars and feeling the mechanical vibrations rumble through him.

'I'd hang on if I were you.' Speaking over his shoulder he twisted the throttle and the engine roared in reply. 'Let's let this old girl off the leash and see what she can do.'

And with a sudden jolt and a screech they were off.

Calista had no choice but to wrap her arms around Lukas's waist as they sped away from the cemetery, leaving its occupants in blissful peace as Lukas navigated the bike onto the coastal road that wound its way round the island. She leant her body into his, the wind whipping her hair back from her face, drying the breath in her throat as she clung on for dear life.

He was driving deliberately fast, she knew that, trying to frighten her, make her squeal. Well, she wasn't nine years old any more, and she certainly wasn't going to give him the satisfaction of behaving as if she was. In fact as soon as they got to the villa she would show him that she didn't intend to take any more of his bullying ways.

The stunning Greek scenery flashed past, the dramatic coastline with its towering cliffs and secluded coves stretching before them. Screwing up her eyes against the glare of the sun sparkling on the sea, Calista knew it wasn't fear she was feeling anyway. It was exhilaration. She felt alive, invigorated, realising how good it was to be back on Thalassa. More than that, realising how much she had missed it.

She adjusted her position slightly and felt Lukas's body respond, the broad width of his back heating against the crush of her breasts, the muscles of his waist shifting beneath the grip of her hands. A dangerous shudder of pleasure went through her. The island wasn't the only thing she had missed. And she was going to have to be very careful about that.

The twisty road took them past the turning for Villa Melina, *her* family villa, and continued east across the top of the island in the direction of Villa Helene— home to Lukas and his father, Stavros, now deceased.

It was a road Calista knew well—probably a distance of six miles or so. She had cycled it many times as a child, frequently seeking out the company of Lukas and his kindly father in preference to her own curmudgeonly father and boring half-brothers, with whom she'd had absolutely nothing in common. But she'd never paid much attention to the names of the two villas before—Melina, the name of Aristotle's first wife and Helene, Lukas's mother. She hadn't known either woman, but it was obvious now she thought about it that the villas had been named after them.

What she *hadn't* known—what no one had known by the look of it—was that Thalassa had actually belonged to them. No one except Lukas, of course, who had used that information to buy the entire island— presumably as a way of getting back at her family. She had no idea what had happened to the Lukas she had once known. What had become of him...

Turning off the coastal road, Lukas bumped the bike up the dirt track that lead to Villa Helene and pulled up in front of the entrance in a spray of dry dust.

Quickly dismounting, he held out his hand to her, but there was nothing gentlemanly about the gesture. It was done with an aggressively urgent air. Shepherding her before him, he unlocked the front door—an action that surprised Calista in itself. *No one* bothered to lock their doors on the island of Thalassa.

Inside, the villa was just as she remembered it. Even the smell was familiar—somehow both comforting and unsettling. She followed Lukas down the cool hallway until they reached the large living room that ran the entire width of the villa. It was still and dark in there, until Lukas strode over to the bi-fold doors, unlocked them and pushed them wide open, undoing the shutters so that the light streamed in.

Calista blinked. The stunning panoramic view of the Aegean Sea appeared before them, but Calista's focus was solely on the room she now saw so clearly. Or, more specifically, on the sofa in the room. The one

she had so recklessly fallen onto with Lukas that evening, in a tangle of fervid, scorching, pumping desire.
The one where Effie had been conceived.

'Drink?' Lukas grabbed a couple of glasses from
the sideboard and reached for a decanter of whisky.

'No, thank you.' Calista dragged her burning eyes
away from the scene of their complete madness.

'Mind if I do?' Pouring himself a generous slug,
he knocked it back in one gulp, then poured another.

Clearly he wasn't waiting for her consent.

Averting her eyes from the sheer brutal beauty of
him, Calista quickly scanned the rest of the familiar
room; the white walls displaying colourful local artwork, the rustic wooden furniture and the travertine
marble flooring. She had always loved this villa. More
so than her own family's, in fact, which Aristotle had
massively extended over the years as a succession of
different women had needed to be impressed and the
urge to display his wealth had become ever more important.

Villa Helene was more modest, more traditionally
Greek, with towering walls affording much needed
shade and the exterior woodwork painted that partic-
ular Mediterranean blue. Not that it lacked any modern comforts, with its large stainless steel kitchen, a
beautiful infinity pool that glistened invitingly through
the open doors, five bedrooms, a gymnasium and a
library. There was even a helipad where, out of the
corner of her eye, Calista had noticed a gleaming helicopter, heating up in the sun as they had walked in.
So *that* was how he had got here…

'So, what is this unfinished business?' She decided to take the lead rather than wait for Lukas like a fly in his web. She watched as he set down his glass, swallowing hard as he started towards where she stood in the middle of the room. 'What is it you want to talk about?'

'The talking can wait.' He stopped before her, towering over her as he gazed down her flushed face. 'Right now I am more interested in action.'

With no warning he reached forward, sliding a hand around the back of her neck, lifting the weight of her hair for a second, before dropping it so that it rippled down her back. 'Right now I want you to kiss me the way you kissed me the last time we were here, *agapi mou*. Do you remember?'

Calista felt herself sway. His hand was branding the back of her neck…his hot, whisky-tinged breath was shooting sharp waves of longing throughout her body. Of course she remembered. She remembered every minuscule, heart-stopping, life-changing detail. She had been living it for the past five years.

It had been her eighteenth birthday party—a gloriously warm June evening. Calista had finished her exams and finally left the boarding school that she had disliked so much, and she'd been intending to soak up a few weeks of Greek sunshine before returning to the UK to start university.

She had been looking forward to the party—not so much to the actual event, the guest list for which had mostly comprised her father's business cronies and their families, rather than her friends, although that had partly been *her* decision. Aristotle had told her to invite as many people as she wanted, offering to pay for their flights from the UK and to put them up at the villa, 'So they can see the sort of wealth you come from.' But she hadn't had that many friends—she'd always been the outsider at school, a motherless red-haired creature with a Greek name—and she hadn't intended to scare off the couple of friends she *had* had by subjecting them to the full force of her father.

Because far from wanting to show off Aristotle's wealth she had been embarrassed by it—or, more precisely, embarrassed by Aristotle. Over the years he had become ever more boorish, more overbearing, and the large quantities of alcohol he'd consumed, along with the banquet-type meals that he demanded every night, had not helped his general health or his temper. It had seemed the larger he'd got, the more obnoxious he'd become.

But there had been one person Calista *had* wanted to see—Lukas. He had promised her that he would be there, and that alone had been enough to see her struggling to straighten her unruly tumble of red hair, carefully applying some lipstick and eyeliner and easing herself into a short emerald-green silk dress that had hugged her youthful curves in just the right places. Donning a pair of strappy gold sandals, complete with killer heels, she had been ready to go—or, more importantly, ready for Lukas.

Except he hadn't showed up.

The disappointment had been crushing. Calista's fragile hopes had been dashed every time another group of guests had appeared and he hadn't been amongst them. It had seemed as if more and more people had come, spilling out onto the terrace, laughing, drinking, dancing...

Finally Lukas's father Stavros had arrived, bursting onto the terrace in a highly agitated state, seeking out Aristotle and demanding that he go inside with him so that they could talk in private. Calista hadn't even had a chance to ask him where Lukas was.

In the end she had decided to take matters into her own hands. Suddenly she had no longer just wanted to *see* Lukas. Being with him had become an all-consuming compulsion, taking on a frightening urgency that would have seen her do almost anything to achieve her aim.

Which had turned out to be stealing a car. Or rather 'borrowing it' from Stavros, who had left the keys of his SUV in the ignition. Calista had only had a handful of driving lessons—she had certainly never passed her driving test—but such had been her determination to see Lukas that she hadn't been about to let a little thing like that stand in her way.

Somehow she had managed to negotiate the twisty coastal road without tumbling the car off the cliff and then, armed with a bottle of champagne and what she hoped was a winning smile, she had burst into Villa Helene and found Lukas anxiously pacing the floor.

He had looked astonished to see her. 'Callie! What on earth are you doing here?'

'I've come to find you, of course. It's my birthday, in case you've forgotten.'

'No, I've not forgotten. Happy Birthday.'

He'd said the requisite words but there had been none of his usual warmth, no kiss on the cheek or birthday hug.

Instead he had looked distractedly over her shoulder. 'Have you seen my father?'

'Yes, he's at my birthday party. Which is where *you* should be. You promised, Lukas.'

'Did he seem okay?'

'Yes—why?'

'It's just that he left here in a hell of a hurry and refused to tell me what was going on.'

'Well, he seemed fine to me.' It had only been a small lie. Calista could have had no idea of the consequences. 'He was chatting with Papa. He told me to come and get you.'

'He gave you the keys to his car?' Clearly puzzled, Lukas had obviously tried to work out what was going on. But Calista hadn't gone there to talk about Stavros. Right up until that moment she hadn't been entirely sure why she *was* there, but suddenly she had known with an all-consuming certainty.

She wanted Lukas to make love to her.

She still remembered his look of surprise as she had moved towards him, the way he had finally smiled when she had flung her arms around his neck, the bottle of champagne still in her hand, clunking heavily against his back. He had laughed, telling her to stop being silly, that she must have had too much to drink, but when he had pulled back to look into her eyes he had seen the truth.

That she wasn't a child any more. That she knew what she was doing. *That she wanted him.*

Even so, he had resisted. But as she had shamelessly pressed her body up against his, chucking the bottle of champagne onto a chair so that she could thread her fingers through his dark curls to pull him closer, she had felt him weaken. And when she had finally claimed his lips, when the first split second of panic and insecurity on her part and complete shock on his had vanished, rapidly melting into desire and then into a burning passion that had seen them stumble backwards onto the sofa, there had been no turning back.

And now they were here again—in the exact same spot. And Calista was horrified to find that the pull of his attraction was just as strong…that she still wanted him every bit as much as she had that June night, even knowing what he had done, even having seen the man he had become.

For Lukas was no longer the warm, funny, laid-back guy she had originally fallen in love with. Along with the dark curls, the mischievous twinkle in his eyes had gone, to be replaced by a cruel stare and a grim determination that sent a shiver down her spine.

And yet still she wanted him.

Her whole body thrummed, all but begging to be his. He was too close—far too close—his head bent so that there was no escaping the searing intensity of his eyes.

'Of course I remember.' She dragged up the words from somewhere, fighting to find some control. 'But, believe me, I won't be making the same mistake again.'

'So it was a *mistake*, was it? That's an interesting choice of word.'

'Yes…yes, it was.' Heat flared in her cheeks.

'Because, you see, *I* don't think it was a mistake at all.' He lowered his head until their lips were only a fraction apart. 'I think it was all very carefully planned.'

'What do you mean?' she whispered hoarsely against the seduction of his mouth.

'And now it's time for my plan to be put into place. My turn to seduce you.'

'No, Lukas, don't be ridiculous!' She tried to pull back but he held her firm.

'And you know what? I have to say I am *very* much looking forward to it.'

Suddenly his mouth was on hers, his hand pushing up through her hair, grasping the back of her head and holding her to him. She was powerless to escape. Even if she had wanted to. Even if she had somehow managed to harness the will-power that had scattered in all directions at the very first touch of his mouth.

His tongue had easily parted her lips and he continued his relentless assault, kissing her with a force driven by need, by hunger and by the dark greed that had clearly overtaken him. It was totally uncompromising, ruthless in its pressure, devastating in its delivery. And impossible to resist.

Because despite everything—despite the whole damned mess of their lives—Calista felt herself melt, dissolve. Molten heat slid through her, unerringly finding its way to her core, where it settled, pulsing hot and deep and hard and relentless. As Lukas continued his skilful assault she found herself leaning in to him, shuddering with pleasure when his hand lowered to the swell of her bottom, tantalisingly skimming over her buttocks before clenching tight in a blatant display of dominance and possession.

She moaned softly, but it was swallowed by Lukas's mouth as he changed the angle of his head so that he could plunder her mouth more deeply, take her completely. His hand flattened, searing into her, pressing her against the thick swell of him. If she had had any resistance before it vanished completely at the shockingly real evidence of his arousal and the deeply carnal response that ricocheted through her body.

He was moving them now, propelling her eager body backwards, one hand still holding her bottom, the other pressed into the small of her back so that he could steer her where he wanted her to go. Together they stumbled as one entwined unit, until Calista felt the wall behind her and realised she had nowhere else to go. Nowhere else she *wanted* to go. Nowhere except into the drugging dark oblivion of Lukas's power.

For a second their eyes met, and Calista felt her breath stall at the darkly savage look that shadowed his handsome face. But then his mouth was on hers again, and she was lost in the rush of sensual need and the burning hunger that shook her entire body.

She felt his hand move to her thigh, lifting her leg over his hip. She wrapped it around him to steady herself, to expose herself more to the pulsing throb of him. She heard his low growl of approval—or maybe it was victory…she didn't have the capacity to tell. His hand pushed up her skirt, his impatient fingers tugging aside the flimsy fabric of her panties so that he could feel her, slide against her, letting out a grunt, a mirthless sort of half-laugh, as he felt her buck against his touch, her shudder of pleasure immediately starting to build and grow.

Quickly pulling away, he released her from his grasp, letting her leg drop to the ground. Feeling in the pocket of his jacket, he took out a condom, ripping open the packet with his teeth at the same time as shrugging off the jacket and unbuttoning his trousers so they fell to the ground. His boxer shorts went next, before he rolled the condom onto himself with one deft movement.

Then he was all hers again, picking up her arms and moving them around his neck, so that when she clung on, holding him as tightly as he knew she would, he was able to lift her off her feet and wait for her legs to wrap around his waist, as he knew they would, her shoes clattering to the floor.

With his free hand he tugged her panties aside again. Only this time it wasn't his finger that nudged against her, it was the head of his arousal—hot and hard and silky and perfectly positioned to sink into her.

It felt like the most erotically glorious promise in the world.

And a second later that promise was delivered.

Suddenly he was inside her, smooth and hard and deep, filling her body and soul, and her every heightened emotion tuned in to nothing except this one incredible moment. Her mew of pleasure turned into a shriek of need, wordlessly commanding him not to stop, to keep going, faster, deeper, to take her to that place she had feared she would never find again.

Which was exactly what he did. Their bodies banged heedlessly against the wall behind them, until Calista could hang on no longer and, screaming out his name, found her shuddering, hollowing release. She felt Lukas stiffen, his body go into a rigid spasm, before he too gave in to the inevitable and roared his surrender into the tangle of her hair.

CHAPTER THREE

PUSHING HIMSELF AWAY from the wall with the palms of his hands, Lukas caged Calista between his locked arms. He wasn't going to give her any more space—not yet. Not while his breath was still heaving in his lungs, his heart hammering in his chest. He stared down at the top of her head, registering the way her slight figure shook, even though she had returned both feet to the floor, rearranging the skirt of her dress as if to pretend nothing had happened.

Well, it had. He had exacted his revenge.

All the hours he had spent plotting and scheming had finally come to fruition. Exactly as he had planned. Exactly on his terms. All done in the name of retribution.

At least that was what he had told himself. But, in truth, lying awake at night and reliving that fateful evening they had spent together had become something of an obsession. And conjuring up Calista's image had not been purely about revenge—far from it. It had become his guilty pleasure. The soft swell of her breasts, the silky touch of her pale skin, her fresh scent, her sweet breath… The memory had transported him from the dismal walls of his cell to a very different place indeed.

He had lost count of the number of times he had travelled the length of her body in his mind, leaving no part of her soft curves untouched by his attentions, and his own body had responded in the most carnal way as he'd listened to the dry snoring of his cellmate in the bunk above him and cursed to hell the situation he had found himself in.

But now he was free. Now he had achieved his goal.

So why wasn't he feeling it? Why wasn't he getting the satisfaction he so badly craved? Why wasn't it enough?

The sex itself had more than lived up to its promise. Just like the first time, there had been something about the connection between them—the chemistry, the fit—that had taken it beyond just sex to another level, as if they had been created solely for the gratification of each other. Not in an easy, comfortable way—not in the way of friends or gentle lovers—but with a wild, dramatic energy.

Like asteroids colliding in the vastness of space, their paths predetermined by a higher being, they had exploded against one another, set each other alight. And ultimately they had blown each other apart.

He could take her again—right here and now—he felt himself harden at the thought of it. In fact he could take her over and over again—keep her here in his villa until he had got her out of his system once and for all. After all, didn't she deserve it after the way she had treated him?

He was halfway to crazily convincing himself it was a good idea when he stopped, looking down at himself. A thirty-one-year-old man, standing there with his pants around his ankles. A man whose desire for the woman in front of him was dangerously close to being out of control.

Perhaps he needed to take a step back to examine his motives. And fast.

Dropping his arms, he wrenched off the condom and quickly disposed of it, then saw to his pants and trousers, buttoning the waistband as he turned away.

'Do you want that drink now?' He spoke over his shoulder, not wanting to look at Calista for fear of what he might see in her eyes. He needed another drink before he could do that.

'Lukas…?'

She whispered his name like a baffled question. The way she might speak to a person she had come across after a very long time—someone who had changed so irrevocably, so much for the worse, that she couldn't be sure it was him. Well, this was him now. And she had better get used to it.

With two glasses of whisky in his hand he turned, bracing himself for what he would see. But still she got to him, those green eyes of hers instantly finding their target, making the glasses clink together in his hand. It was a look of turmoil—of confusion and hurt and something Lukas refused to acknowledge, let alone try to analyse.

He had made her feel bad. But hadn't that been

his intention? He refused to let his conscience prick him now.

Striding towards her, he handed her a glass, noticing the way her hand shook as she reached for it, immediately raising it to her lips to take a sip. The whisky seemed to restore her, and the flush of colour in her cheeks lessened from feverish red to a gentle pink.

'Yes, Calista?' He returned her question with the mocking sarcasm built up over five bitter years. He saw her flinch.

'Whatever has happened to you?'

'Let me see…' He pretended to consider. 'Lies, betrayal, deceit, the death of my father, and…oh, yes, four and a half years rotting in an Athens jail.'

He watched as she shook her head. 'I have no idea who you are any more, Lukas. Do you know that?'

'No? Well, maybe that makes two of us.' He took a deep slug of whisky. 'And yet *still* you let me push you up against a wall and have my way with you. Why is that, do you suppose?'

'I… I don't know.'

'*Still* you come apart at the very first touch of my hands, urging me on as if you can't get enough of me, screaming my name as you take what you so badly need from me.'

This felt better—dishing out the punishment he knew she deserved.

'And you are still dressed in black, your dear, departed father scarcely cold in his grave. It's hardly becoming, is it, Calista? It's hardly fitting behaviour for a grieving daughter.'

'No, it's not. It should never have happened. And, believe me, I regret it now.'

'Oh, I'm sure you do. But that doesn't mean it won't happen again.' He closed the space between them with one menacing step. 'Because you and I both know, Calista, that I can have you any time I want, any place I want.'

He watched the way his words inflicted pain, sawed away at her just the way he'd intended them to. But with the pain came adrenalin, swiftly followed by that glorious flash of temper.

'So *that's* what all this is about, is it?' She threw back her shoulders, her hair rippling down her back. 'You have lured me here to prove that you can have sex with me in some sort of pathetic attempt to get your own back?'

'Something like that.'

She opened her mouth, but for a second words failed her. 'You are a despicable, vile creature—do you know that? A lousy piece of—'

'Yeah, yeah.' He shut her down with a bored flick of his wrist. 'I'm sure I'm all that and more. You can call me all the names you want, if it makes you feel better, but it won't change the facts. And do you know what the worst of it is?'

He let his eyes drift lazily over her outraged face.

'You didn't even put up a fight. I had been looking forward to the challenge, the thrill of the chase, to working out how I was going to win you over. But in the end it was so easy it was almost pathetic.'

It was as if he'd punched her. The shock of his words

made her fold at the stomach, reach for the back of a chair beside her to stop herself from falling. Raking in a breath, she pulled herself upright. Then, shooting him one last look of utter revulsion, she turned to go.

With lightning speed Lukas reached the doorway before her, easily barring her way. 'Not so fast.'

'I would like you to move, please.' Her voice was brittle with anger and hurt.

'Uh-uh. You will leave when *I* say so.'

'Is this part of your master plan?' She put her hands on her hips, as if to try and anchor herself. 'To hold me against my will? Keep me here as your prisoner so that you can prove just what a detestable macho bully you have become?'

'And supposing I did?' Lukas arrowed her a lethal look. 'You and I both know what would happen. You would be all over me, Calista. Oh, you might pretend to be outraged…put up a display of resistance in the name of decorum. But in truth I would only have to click my fingers and you would be mine. Writhing beneath me, on top of me, down on me, begging for my attentions and then screaming for more. Look how you behaved just now. It's pitiful, really. I should feel sorry for you.'

Slap.

The weight of Calista's palm connected with the side of his jaw with an impressive crack.

He had seen it coming. He could have stopped it. Spending time amongst some of Greece's most notorious criminals had honed his instincts, taught him to read the situation before it happened. Lukas had always had fast reactions—now they were razor-sharp. But for some reason he had let it happen. For some reason he had wanted to feel it—that burn, that most primitive connection—to show that he was alive. To show that he could get to her. And the sting from her palm *had* set his heart racing.

Calista Gianopoulous—the young woman he hadn't been able to get out of his mind, whose betrayal had consumed him so obsessively that it had become part of the fabric of who he was. Now he had her where he wanted her. Now her humiliation was in his grasp. And he could squeeze as tightly as he wished.

He studied her intently, standing there with her chin held high, her breasts heaving seductively beneath the demure black dress, pulling the fabric tight with every gasping, defiant breath. Her eyes flashed with a green so intense, so wild, it was as if she had been stripped of her sanity.

He should be feeling vindicated, triumphant. But he didn't feel either of those things. Instead he was simply consumed with the overwhelming need to possess her body again. His only conscious thought was how utterly magnificent she looked.

He let a second of silence pass and tried to pull himself together, waiting to see what she would do next—almost willing her to strike him again so that this time he could intercept it, grasp her wrist and feel that physical connection between them again, see where it might lead. But instead she let her hand drop by her side, lowering the tawny sweep of her lashes. The pink pout of her lower lip, he noticed, had started to quiver.

'Resorting to violence, Calista?' He gave a derisive laugh. 'I would never have thought it of you.'

'It's no more than you deserve.'

'No? Maybe not. But if we're dishing out home truths, perhaps it's time that you took a look at yourself.'

Her head came up and there was fear in her eyes. 'What do you mean by that?'

'Oh, come on, Calista, let's drop the pretence. You see, I *know*.'

'Kn…know what?'

If Lukas had had any doubt about her part in his downfall it was well and truly dispelled now. Guilt was written all over her pretty face—not just written, but spelled out in big, bold capitals. She positively shook with it, her hands trembling as she raised them to her mouth, her legs looking as if they wouldn't be able to hold her up much longer.

He let out a grim laugh. 'Do you *really* need me to spell it out for you?'

'Lukas… I…'

'Because I will if you want.'

Taking a couple of steps away he then turned, his eyes pinning her to the spot, as if they were in a courtroom.

'Let me take you back to the night of your eighteenth birthday party. The night my father discovered that the police had boarded one of the ships and found it was loaded with arms. While Stavros was over at Villa Melina, trying to find out what the hell was going on, *your* father dispatched you to "entertain" me. And you did a magnificent job—I have to say that.'

He paused, his whole body brittle with seething contempt.

'Aristotle must have been very proud of you. While my father was suffering a heart attack you were in full seduction mode...while people were mobilising a helicopter to get him to the mainland we were in the throes of passion. And by the time they got him there it was too late.'

'*No*, Lukas.' Calista bit down hard on her quivering lip. 'It wasn't like that.'

'Oh, but it *was*, Calista. It was *exactly* like that. Before my father had the chance to confront yours, to defend himself, he conveniently had a heart attack and died. I bet Aristotle couldn't believe his luck.'

'That's...that's an awful thing to say.'

'It was an *awful* deed.' He mocked her use of the totally inadequate word. 'Not only was he profiting from his vile trade in arms, but when he got caught out he set up *my* father to take the blame. He betrayed his oldest friend. It doesn't get much more *awful* than that.'

'No! I don't believe you!' Calista let out a cry of anguish. 'My father had nothing to do with the arms-smuggling. And he would never have betrayed Stavros.'

'And I don't suppose he was responsible for getting me arrested and banged up in jail for four and a half years either?' Lukas gave a harsh laugh.

'No! I don't believe that either. How would that even have been possible?'

'Remarkably easily, as it turned out. It seems your father had villainous friends in remarkably high places. Or should I say *low* places?'

'No! You're making all this up.'

'Don't insult my intelligence by pretending you didn't know.' Lukas ran a hand over his close-cropped hair. 'No doubt you have tried to dress it up over the years—reshape your traitorous actions to ease your conscience, help you sleep at night. But the fact is you betrayed me in the same way your father betrayed *my* father. You traded your innocence for my guilt. I just hope it was a price worth paying.'

Calista turned away from him, stumbling across the room towards the open doors of the terrace. She clearly couldn't face him—well, that was hardly surprising. He stared at her silhouette, dark against the azure blue of the sea meeting the sky. He could feel the thrum of his pulse in his ears, a tightness in his chest that had yet to be released.

He wasn't done with her yet.

'So you see, *agape mou*, this is my little payback. My turn to let you see what it's like to be used. To be taken advantage of. To have your body violated by someone for their own gain.'

Closing the gap between them, he placed a hand on her shoulder, turning her so that she couldn't avoid the hard, dark glitter of his eyes.

'So tell me, Calista. How does it feel?'

Calista tried to swallow past the shock that was blocking her throat. Her heart was thudding wildly in her chest, her palm still stinging from where it had connected with Lukas's jaw. But her brain had gone into slow motion, struggling to process all the terrible things he had said.

Her father had been responsible for the arms-smuggling scandal? He had somehow pinned the blame on Stavros, and then Lukas? And Lukas thought she was part of the conspiracy plot.

It was all too much. She suddenly felt dizzy, clammy. But at least he didn't know about Effie...

Dragging in a breath, Calista made herself focus on the one small speck of relief amid these horrendous revelations.

For one heart-stopping moment she had thought she'd got it wrong—that he had known all along. She had been on the brink of blurting it out—getting in first before he could use it as some sort of weapon against her. Because that was undoubtedly what he wanted to do—hurt her. But hadn't he already done that a thousand times without even trying?

But, no, it wasn't Effie he was talking about. It was all about *her*—how she had betrayed him, used him, somehow been responsible for his downfall. It seemed he had brought her here solely to humiliate her. Setting a trap to lure her into having sex with him as some sort of payback. And she had leapt right in.

The shame of it shuddered through her, right down to her core, which still throbbed where he had been, where she had let him possess her. No, not *let* him— encouraged him, urged, pleaded, begged... She could hear her breathless entreaties as he had taken her, devoured her, driving into her with a raging desire that had consumed them both, obliterating all reason.

Now her reckless words scraped across her skin like sandpaper. It was bad enough that she had fallen so wantonly into his arms. But for it all to have been a trap...? A wave of sickness engulfed her.

She ran a shaky hand over her forehead, pushing back the hair that was sticking to her forehead. She had to get away from here—back to Villa Melina, where she had left her overnight bag, and then across to the mainland so she could catch a flight back to the UK.

She stepped out onto the terrace, squinting against the light, not knowing whether Lukas would try and stop her, no longer having any idea what he was capable of. She could feel his cruel eyes boring into her, following her every movement.

'Nothing to say, Calista?' he called mockingly after her.

'Only that I'm leaving.' She hurled the words over her shoulder.

'No grovelling apology, then? No promises that you will somehow make it up to me?'

'*I* have nothing to apologise for.' She turned on her heel, determined to fire one last parting shot. '*You* are the one who needs to take responsibility for what you did.'

'Have you not understood a word I said?' He was right behind her now, his dark shadow engulfing her. 'Or are the lies so deeply ingrained that you have started to believe them yourself? I had nothing to do with the arms-smuggling. My father had nothing to do with the arms-smuggling. The only person responsible for the whole deadly disgrace was your father—Aristotle Gianopoulous.'

'No!' Calista spun around, focussing on channelling her outrage rather than having to face the awful prospect of letting herself believe it. Because there *was* that niggle of doubt…that worm of suspicion crawling up her spine.

'*Yes*, Calista.'

'But the court case…' Her voice began to crack. 'Stavros was proved to be guilty… You were proved to be implicated.'

'I've told you—it was all a set-up. A couple of corrupt lawyers, someone high up in the police department, a good forger and a few fake witnesses. You'd be amazed what money can buy if you offer enough of it. And at the time Aristotle was positively awash with it—his hands stained red with the blood money that had passed through them. He'd never get away with it now, of course.' He paused for effect. 'Now I too know the right people, and I am fully conversant with the way these things work. But at the time I was naïve enough to think that justice would prevail.'

Calista covered her face with her hands. She desperately didn't want it to be true, desperately wanted to be able to defend her father. But something about the steady look in Lukas's eyes, the flat, leaden tone of his voice, made it impossible not to believe him.

Suddenly the truth of it struck her like a blow to the chest.

'A pretty performance.' Like a big cat stalking its prey, Lukas held himself very still, as if ready to strike with the killer pounce. 'Are you trying to tell me you didn't know?'

'No, Lukas, I didn't know.' Her voice was barely more than a whisper from behind her hands.

'Sadly the evidence doesn't support your claim.' He inched closer. 'What brought you to Villa Helene that night, if not orders to keep me out of the way?'

'I wanted to see you—that's all.' She let her hands fall from her face, looking down at her feet to avoid Lukas's punishing stare.

'Hmm... I'm afraid you're going to have to do better than that. Much better. Because you were a girl on a mission that night, dressed to kill, and I was your unwitting prey. That whole seduction routine was totally out of character. Why exactly *was* that, Calista, unless you were following your father's orders?'

'I'm telling you—my father knew nothing about it. It was my birthday, and I wanted to spend it with you.'

'But *why*, Calista?'

A beat of silence passed before Calista dragged in a breath. She might as well say it. What did it matter any more? What did *any* of it matter?

'Because I was in love with you, of course.' She uttered the words with a quiet, despondent clarity. 'I'd been in love with you ever since I turned thirteen—before that, even.'

Reaching for her chin, Lukas tipped up her face so that he could see into her eyes, searching for the truth. 'But you were just a kid.'

'And that's exactly what I was trying to do.' She blinked against his stare. 'Prove that I wasn't a kid any more.'

She saw his jaw clench as he assimilated this information, his brows lowering into a considering scowl.

'And you expect me to *believe* that?' When he finally spoke his voice was as dark as the night. 'You expect me to believe that it is pure coincidence that you offered yourself to me at the exact same time as my father was confronting Aristotle? In an exchange so heated, so monumental, that the stress of it took my father's life?'

'Do you know what, Lukas?' Calista let out a jagged breath. 'I really don't care what you believe.'

All she could think about was getting away while her legs still had the ability to carry her. Somehow she had to process the shock of her father's guilt, but she couldn't do that here—not on top of the shame of what had just happened with Lukas, not with him standing over her like this, all dark, menacing force.

Turning away, she set off across the terrace, intending to go around the side of the villa and make her way up to the road so she could find her way back to Villa Melina. If she was lucky she might come across Petros in his battered old car. If not she would walk. Anything would be better than staying here to be verbally abused by Lukas.

But she had taken no more than a couple of steps before Lukas had headed her off, blocking her way with the powerful wall of his honed physique.

'Not so fast.' His hair shone blue-black in the sunshine, sharp shadows highlighting the stark angles of his cheeks and jaw. 'I'm not done with you yet.'

'Well, I'm done with *you*. Get out of my way.'

'You didn't really think I would fall for that pathetic *"but I loved you, Lukas"* routine, did you?'

Calista flinched, her body hollowed out by the cruelty of his words. *'Loved,* Lukas. Firmly in the past tense. Now I loathe your guts.'

'Ah, that's more like it. Now we're getting to the truth. And, for the record, I know exactly why you're so desperate to get away, to run back to the cosy little world you have created for yourself in England. *Guilt,* Calista. No matter what you say, how you try and wriggle out of it, your guilt is written all over your face.'

He was right, of course. Calista knew—the guilt he was talking about—she could feel it gripping the muscles of her face, clenching her abdomen. But it wasn't the kind of guilt Lukas thought it was. It had nothing to do with luring him to have sex with her. It was about Effie, and the very real consequences of that fateful night. The fact that Lukas had a daughter he knew nothing about. She knew she would have to tell him. Just not here—not now. Right now she didn't have the strength.

'Perhaps you're mistaking the look on my face.' Still she fought to stand her ground. Because fighting for survival was what she did. What she had always done. 'It's not guilt I feel—it's shame.'

'Guilt, shame—call it whatever you like.' He moved closer, as if scenting a kill. 'Either way I am pleased to see you accepting responsibility for your actions.'

'Oh, I do. I can't ignore what just happened between us—much as I would like to. Because that's the shame

I'm talking about, Lukas—the shame I feel for having let you touch me, violate me.'

'Ha!' He let out a cruel laugh. 'So I *violated* you, did I? Was that before or after you wrapped yourself around me, screaming my name in pleasure?'

'I *hate* you, Lukas!'

'Yeah, yeah—so you keep saying. Who are you trying to convince? Me or you? Because you should know that I don't give a damn.'

His eyes narrowed dangerously, glinting as some new idea occurred to him. Calista felt a fresh wave of alarm.

'Or is there another reason you're so desperate to get away, to pin the blame on me?' His voice was as sharp as the edge of a blade. 'Are you seeing someone? Is that it? Do you have a boyfriend, a lover?'

Suddenly the air stilled. The sun that was beating down on them was stiflingly hot. The force of his question felt like a hand around her throat.

'If I did it would be none of your business.' Calista twisted her head as if to dislodge the imaginary grasp, clinging on to her defiance like a shield to protect herself.

'Is *that* why you can't look me in the eye, Calista?' His voice became ever more urgent, more demanding. 'Is *that* why you're so desperate to apportion blame, to make me out to be the bad guy?'

'No. That has nothing to do with it.'

'Then tell me it's not true.'

Clasping hold of her wrist, Lukas held it in his grasp.

'Very well.' She indignantly tried to snatch back her hand, but Lukas held on. 'I do not have a lover, Lukas.'

'A boyfriend, then? A partner of some description?'

'No, none of those things. Now, kindly let me go.'

'What, then? Tell me. Because I can *see* it, Calista. I can see it in your eyes.'

Calista hesitated. She could feel the moment closing in on her, weighing down on her with leaden pressure. Suddenly there was no escape.

'I do not have a lover, Lukas.' She summoned the words from deep inside her, where the truth had lain dormant for so long. 'But I *do* have a child.'

'A child?' He dropped her arm as if it were made of molten metal. 'You have a *child*?'

'Yes.' She watched as the shock that had contorted his handsome features settled into a brutal grimace of stone. 'I have a four-and-a-half-year-old daughter.'

She paused, sucking in a breath as if it might be her last.

This was it.

'And so, Lukas, do you.'

CHAPTER FOUR

LUKAS STARED AT Calista in frozen, abject horror. No, it couldn't be true. He couldn't *possibly* have fathered a child.

But of course he could. They had had sex—unprotected sex, he recalled with blistering clarity. At the time he had been too astonished, too blown away by the turn of events, even to think about taking precautions. And since that evening he had never given it another thought.

He reined in the emotions that were ricocheting around his head like gunfire and forced himself to think logically. Calista was a scheming, manipulative piece of work—he already knew that. So what was to say she wasn't making this up? Perhaps there was no daughter, or if there were the child wasn't his?

But, much as he wanted to believe either of those versions as fact—any version that meant this was all a pack of lies—the contortion of Calista's face said it all. She looked sick, visibly paling beneath her creamy white skin. She looked as if she wanted to stuff the reckless words back down her throat.

She looked horrified that she had just revealed a deeply hidden truth.

'Sit down.' He pulled out a metal chair, physically lowering her into it before she collapsed in front of him or toppled into the pool, which was only a few feet away. 'So, let me get this straight. You are telling me that I have fathered a child?'

'Yes.'

He saw her painful swallow.

'And you have only just seen fit to tell me about this?'

'You have been in prison, Lukas.'

'Don't you think I *know* that?' Fury roared in his voice...his hands clenched into fists. Calista flinched. 'But that was no reason not to tell me that I was a father.'

'I thought it best to wait...until you were released.'

'Did you, indeed?' Sarcasm ripped through his voice. 'Best for whom, exactly?'

Calista lowered her head.

'So who else knows? Your family? Aristotle? I'm sure he must have enjoyed being a doting grandfather to my child.'

'No, I didn't tell him. I've told no one.'

Lukas hoped this was true—for Calista's sake.

'So what's her name, this daughter of mine?'

'Effie.'

'Effie?' He snarled the name.

'Short for Euphemia.'

'And where is she now?'

'At home in England.'

'Does she know about me?'

He fired the questions at her as they came into his head, not caring in the least about the way they were making Calista wince, shrink into herself.

'I've told her that you live in a different country. Too far away to visit.'

'Well, we will just have to put that right, won't we?'

Raking a hand through his hair, Lukas let his eyes travel over the smooth turquoise water of the pool before swinging them back to Calista's lowered head. His decision was made.

'I want to see her. As soon as possible. I want my daughter brought over here right away—right now.'

'What?' She looked aghast.

'I will have the jet put on standby.' He checked his watch. 'She could be here by this evening.'

'This evening?' Calista gaped. 'You're not seriously expecting me to fly to the UK, pick up Effie and then fly back with her, just like that?'

'No.'

'Well, thank God for that.' Her shoulders dropped.

'*You* are going nowhere. I am keeping you here until I have seen for myself that my orders have been obeyed and the child has been safely delivered to me.'

'Don't be ridiculous!' she shrieked with alarm. 'Effie is four years old. You can't put her on a plane by herself.'

'My staff will take care of her.'

'No, she would be terrified! I won't allow it!'

'I'm not asking for your permission, Calista.' His voice roared around them. 'Your shameful deceit means that I have already missed four and a half years of my daughter's life. I don't intend to miss any more.'

'Well, think of Effie, then.' Real panic clawed at her throat. 'Please! She's never even been on a plane. She would be completely traumatised by having to travel on her own with a group of strangers. You don't know what she's like…how sensitive she is.'

'You are right.' He saw the flicker of relief on her face, savouring the moment before he twisted the knife still further. 'I *don't* know what she's like.' The look of relief vanished as she realised where he was going with this. 'And whose fault is that?'

She lowered her eyes, then suddenly sat up straight as a thought occurred to her. 'Anyway, Effie can't travel abroad—she doesn't have a passport.'

'Is this another of your lies, Calista? Because if it is…'

'No, it's the truth.'

'Very well.' The synapses in his brain were firing wildly as they adjusted to every new piece of information. 'You and I will fly to England together. That way you can introduce me to my daughter personally.' He met Calista's horrified gaze full-on. 'I will tell my pilot to have the jet ready within the hour.'

Despite his best efforts, by the time they finally pulled up outside Calista's London home dawn was breaking on a new day. The journey had been frustratingly slow. Whisking Calista from Thalassa to the mainland by helicopter hadn't been a problem, but his private jet had had to undergo a series of safety checks before it had been fit to fly.

Apart from a brief period when it had been impounded by the police, before being found legally to belong to Lukas, it had been languishing for years in a hangar at Athens airport, with no one thinking to service it. Lukas had not taken this news well. Now he was out of prison things were going to change—*that* was for sure.

Pulling up outside Calista's house in the car he'd hired from the airport, he craned his neck to take a look. It seemed reasonable enough—a three-storey Victorian terrace on a quiet narrow street.

Beside him Calista was fumbling in her bag for her keys. She had barely spoken to him on the journey here, nor during their long wait at the airport in Athens, or the night flight to London. Not that he cared. He had needed the space to get his head around this astonishing development. To try and work out how to proceed.

Calista had eventually agreed to his suggestion to use the bedroom on the plane, but by the look of her she hadn't had much sleep. Dark circles shadowed her eyes.

'We need to go in quietly. Effie will still be asleep. And Magda.'

Magda, he had managed to ascertain, was some friend of Calista's who shared the house and helped look after Effie. He would be checking *her* out too, making sure she was a suitable person to be around his daughter. Although it was probably a bit late for that. Bitterness had him clenching his fists.

Calista let them into a hallway that was cluttered with bicycles, a child's scooter and a pile of unwanted post.

'Follow me—we're on the top floor.'

'You don't own the whole house?'

'I don't *own* any of it, Lukas,' she hissed over her shoulder as she climbed the stairs. 'I rent the flat. And I can only afford to do that because I share the cost with Magda.'

Lukas remained silent, straining for the sound of imaginary violins. If she imagined he was going to feel sorry for her she had another thought coming. Besides, he was annoyingly distracted by the sight of her bottom as she climbed the stairs ahead of him. Firm and rounded, it moved seductively beneath the tight jeans that she had changed into when she had collected her stuff from Villa Melina.

'Here we are.'

Inserting the key in the lock, Calista pushed open the door and switched on the light in the narrow corridor. She led him into a kitchen. For a second they stood, staring at each other. Lukas felt too big—out of place in this small but tidy space.

'Cal?' A muffled voice came from down the corridor. 'Is that you?'

'Yes,' Calista answered in a hushed whisper, then turned to Lukas. 'I'm going to speak to Magda. Do you want to make yourself some coffee or something?'

She opened a cupboard and quickly took out a bag of ground coffee, thrusting it into his hands and pointing to the cafetière next to the kettle.

'Do it quietly.'

Lukas filled the kettle, looking out over the London rooftops at the pigeons as he waited for it to boil. Twenty-four hours ago there had been no way he would have expected to find himself here.

'Hello.'

A small but very clear voice had him spinning his head around. A young girl with tousled dark curls and sleepy green eyes was standing in the doorway staring at him.

His daughter.

'Who are you?' She looked at him curiously.

'Lukas. Lukas Kalanos.' Lukas stepped forward with his hand outstretched, then dropped it again, feeling inordinately foolish.

'I'm Effie.'

'Um…yes, I know.'

'That is actually short for Euphemia.' Deciding that this man was clearly no match for her social skills, Effie took the initiative. 'I'm four and a half. How old are you?'

'I'm…er…thirty-one.'

Effie stared at him, as if considering such a great age. 'Mummy is twenty-three and Magda is twenty-three too. But Magda is older than Mummy because her birthday comes first.'

'Right. Um…do you want to go and get your mummy?'

'I can't do that, silly. Mummy has gone to Greece to say goodbye to my grandpa. I've never met him. He's dead. D'you want some juice?'

Dragging over a chair, she climbed up to open the

fridge door. She was peering inside when Calista re-appeared.

'Effie?'

'Mummy!' Slamming the fridge door closed, she launched herself at her mother, winding her skinny legs around Calista's waist and hugging her tight. 'You're back! I've missed you *so* much!'

'I've missed you too, my darling.'

'I have actually been brave, though. You can ask Magda.'

'I'm sure you have.'

Kissing the top of her head, Calista extricated herself from the arms and legs and set her down on the floor, holding on to her hand very tightly.

'I see you've met Lukas.'

'Yes. He's thirty-one.'

'Yes.' Calista shot him a glance. 'I expect you're wondering what he's doing here.'

'Maybe he's lost?' Effie offered helpfully.

'No, Effie, he's not lost. He's come here to meet you.'

'Oh!' Effie looked at him with renewed interest.

'The thing is, Effie…we have something to tell you. Why don't you come here and sit on my lap?'

Scraping back a chair, Calista sat down, bringing Effie with her. Lukas was struck by how close they were—not just physically, although with Effie's arm hooked around her mother's neck and her little py-jama-clad body pressed right up against her a whisper couldn't have got between them—but emotionally. They seemed bonded together, like a single unit.

Under different circumstances it would have been

a delight to behold. Now it just made Lukas feel even more of an outsider. Even more incensed by the situation.

'The reason Lukas has come here is because we want to tell you...'

Effie's big green eyes looked from one to the other.

'The thing is... Well, the fact is, what we have to tell you is...'

'I am your father, Euphemia.'

Lukas's voice boomed around the small room, sounding far louder, far more aggressive than he had meant it to. He watched Effie's eyes widen with astonishment before Calista pulled her close, her own eyes blazing with anger.

'*Lukas!*'

'What?' Pushing himself away from the worktop, he drew himself up to his full height. 'The child needs to know.'

In his determination to take control of the situation, not to be painted as the bad guy, it seemed he had managed to do just that. With Effie hugged against her chest Calista started to rock slightly, as if trying and take away the pain. But Effie was struggling to be freed and, finally extricating herself, she stared at him, tucking her hair behind her ear in a gesture that so mimicked Calista it took his breath away.

'Is he telling the truth, Mummy?' Clearly she didn't trust him any more than her mother did.

'Yes—yes, he is, darling. I wish we had broken it to you a little more gently, but Lukas *is* your daddy.'

Sitting up straighter now, Effie reached for the

comfort of Calista's hair, twiddling a curl between her fingers. 'Will he be coming to live here with us and Magda?'

'*No!*' Calista and Lukas chorused together.

'Lukas lives in Greece—where I have just been.'

'With my dead grandpa?'

'Well, sort of…'

'Was he very sad that Grandpa died too?'

'Um…tell you what—why don't you run along and get some clothes on? Then we can all have breakfast together and we'll talk about everything. How about that?'

Effie had barely left the room before Calista rounded on Lukas, eyes blazing. 'What the *hell* do you think you were doing?' She snarled under her breath. 'We agreed we were going to break it to her gently and then you go and blurt it out without any warning.'

'*You* agreed. Besides, you were taking too long about it.'

'Too long! I'd barely had two minutes with her!'

'Well, it's done now. She seems fine with it.'

'And you'd *know*, would you?'

'I know she needs to be told the truth. You have deceived her for long enough.'

'It wasn't deceiving her—I was protecting her.'

'Don't give me that. The only person you were protecting was yourself. It's time the child learnt some decent values that don't involve a web of lies.'

'How *dare* you criticise the way I have raised my daughter?'

'*My* daughter too, Calista. Just remember that.'

'Here I am!'

Effie reappeared in the doorway. She was wearing a stripy tee shirt, some sort of skirt made from pink netting and red wellington boots.

'Well done, darling.' Calista turned to smile at her. 'What would you like for breakfast?'

'I've got a better idea.'

Suddenly Lukas was desperate to get out of the stifling atmosphere of this cramped flat.

'Why don't I take us all out for breakfast?'

'Ooh!' Effie's eyes shone with surprise. 'Can I have a doughnut?'

'You certainly can. As many doughnuts as you like.'

Effie looked from him to her mother and back again, not able to believe her luck. When Calista remained silent a huge smile spread across her face.

Lukas puffed out his chest. Round one to him and the doughnut. It might only be a small victory, but it felt good.

'Faster! Faster!'

Calista looked across the small park to where Lukas was pushing Effie on the roundabout. Her daughter had her head thrown back and her eyes closed, her dark curls streaming out behind her. To the casual observer they might look like any father and daughter, enjoying some time together in the sunshine, but Calista could see the hitch in Lukas's shoulders, the tightness in his jaw as he whirled the roundabout round with one strong hand, the other thrust deep into the pocket of trousers.

Breakfast had been taken at the outside seating area

of a café in Hyde Park. Effie's choice, as it was close
to a children's playground and the boating lake—two
of her favourite things. Effie had valiantly fought her
way through two and a half doughnuts and Lukas
had watched in smug silence, presumably waiting for
Calista to react—which she had refused to do.

She wasn't going to get involved in petty point-scor-
ing. Not when there were so many much bigger issues
at stake. And besides, if he carried on whizzing Effie
round at that speed there was a good chance that nature would score the point for her—preferably all over
his immaculate designer suit.

She took another sip of her third cup of coffee. This
was so bizarre—it simply didn't feel real. The three
of them, here in a London park, with Lukas knowing
about Effie and Effie having finally met her father.
This enormous guilty secret had been in the back of
her mind for so long, gnawing away at her, that it felt
like a living part of her.

She had always known that at some point she was
going to have to tell them both the truth. It was one of
the many things that could keep her awake on those
nights when her troubles seemed to pile in and sleep
refused to come.

Now it had happened. But as she gazed across at
the two of them Calista could feel no sense of relief,
no lifting of the burden she had carried for so long.
Instead a dark thread of dread wound its way through
her, pulling ever tighter as she studied the two of them
together.

Lukas had changed so much from the funny, easy-going, generous young man she had fallen in love with. He was a different person now. Cold, calculating, ruthless. A man who would stop at nothing to get what he wanted.

The roundabout slowed to allow a young boy to get on, and Calista saw the boy's mother—or nanny, maybe—eyeing Lukas, moving closer to say something, giving a little laugh and tossing back her head.

She heard Effie's bossy little voice taking command of the situation as the boy scrambled on. 'You will have to hold tight. My daddy's a fast pusher.'

My daddy. Was it really possible that Effie had accepted Lukas just like that? And, if so, why did that only increase Calista's sense of deep unease?

A few minutes later Effie came running back towards her, her eyes shining, the little boy close behind her.

'Can I go on the slide with Noah, please?'

'Yes, that's fine. I'll watch from here.'

The two of them scampered off and Calista raised her eyes to see the woman with Noah looking at her with disappointment. They smiled politely at one another as Lukas came to sit beside her and the woman turned to follow the children.

'More coffee?' Lukas looked round to call the waitress over.

'No, thanks. In fact we should probably be thinking about leaving.'

'Have plans for the day, do you?' He smiled at the waitress as she took his order for another espresso, making her blush prettily. But his words were weighted with sarcasm.

'And what if I do?' Calista leapt to the challenge. 'Effie and I *do* have a life, you know. A good one, in fact. I have made sure of that. I have done everything in my power to ensure that she is happy and secure, that she wants for nothing.'

'Apart from a father, of course.' Lukas stirred sugar into his coffee and raised the cup to his lips.

Calista scowled.

'Luckily I am in a position to be able to rectify that now.'

'Well, that's as may be.' Calista pursed her lips. 'But don't start thinking you can come storming in and take over our lives. Effie is settled—happy. The last thing she needs is a lot of disruption.'

Slowly replacing his cup on the saucer, Lukas raised heavy-lidded eyes. 'The sooner you start to realise who calls the shots around here, the better it will be for all of us.'

'*I* call the shots.' She could feel a flush creeping up her neck—indignation mixed with righteousness and something horribly like panic. 'Where Effie is concerned, *I* make the decisions.'

'Uh-uh. Not any more, *thespinis mou*.'

With her heart thumping painfully in her chest, Calista turned to see Effie waving madly at them from the top of the slide. She waved back and then Effie pointed at Lukas.

'She wants you to wave.' She forced the words through gritted teeth.

Lukas raised a hand and a purposeful Effie launched herself down the slide.

'So what is it, this life you are so determined to protect?' Lukas's all-seeing gaze swung back in her direction.

'I've told you—it's just a normal life, me and Effie.'

'Tell me about it. Do you work? Does Effie go to school?'

'Effie has just finished pre-school. And I'm about to graduate, as a matter of fact.'

'Graduate in what subject?'

'I've been training to be a nurse for the past three years.'

'A *nurse*?' Clearly this had taken him by surprise.

'Yes.' On safer ground now, Calista pushed back her shoulders. She was proud of her achievement. 'It's been hard, trying to fit it around Effie, but luckily I met Magda. She's on the same course as me and she's been such a huge help. I couldn't have done it without her.'

'So you work where? In a hospital?'

'Not yet. I have to wait for my certificate to come through before I can apply for jobs. I'm going to try and co-ordinate it so that I start work in September, when Effie begins full-time school.'

This information was met with narrowed eyes, absorbed, processed and filed away.

'And Greece? Thalassa? You say Effie has never even been there?'

'No.'

'Why *is* that?'

'Because there has been no need. Greece is no longer a part of my life. I would never have gone back myself if it hadn't been for my father's funeral.'

'And yet you gave our daughter a Greek name?'

'Well, yes.' Calista wasn't sure herself why she had done that. Somehow it had just felt right. 'But that's only because it's a pretty name.'

'Nonsense. You are half-Greek… Euphemia is three-quarters Greek. You both have Greek blood running through your veins, pumping in your heart—it makes you who you are. Do you *really* believe you can dismiss it as easily as that?'

'Well, no, but—'

'Greece will always be a part of your life, whether you want it to be or not. And it will certainly be a part of Effie's. *I* intend to see to that.'

A chilling calm settled over his handsome features, pulling the skin taut against his cheekbones, holding his handsome head high.

A trickle of dread seeped into Calista's veins. 'What do you mean by that?'

'I mean that I have no intention of missing any more of my daughter's life. I am going to take Effie back to Thalassa with me.'

'No! No, Lukas, you *can't*…'

'Yes, Calista, I can. Either she comes on her own or you accompany her. The choice is yours. But either way my daughter *will* return to Thalassa with me.'

CHAPTER FIVE

As THE HELICOPTER blades whirled to a stop Calista watched Lukas flick off the controls and unbuckle his seatbelt. Less than twenty-four hours had passed and they were back at Villa Helene, just as he had decreed.

He had won.

There was no way she would have let Effie travel to Thalassa without her—the idea was unthinkable. So instead she had tried to reason with him, suggesting they paid a visit at a later date, or that perhaps Lukas could stay in London for a while and get to know his daughter slowly. But Lukas had had none of it. Even Calista's trump card—that Effie didn't have a passport—had been swept aside, and a visit to the passport office had been arranged and completed with scary efficiency.

So there had been nothing for it. Calista had had to agree.

She looked down at Effie, who was sound asleep in her arms. The journey to Thalassa was a long and tiring one when you were only four, and Effie's huge excitement had finally given way to sleep on the final leg of their journey. She had been nestling into her mother's lap and closing her eyes before the helicopter had even left the mainland.

Now Lukas turned to face them, his expression closed, businesslike.

'I have instructed Petros and Dorcas to make the villa ready for us. I imagine Effie will want to be put straight to bed?'

Calista nodded. 'Yes, she's exhausted.'

Petros and Dorcas. They were working for Lukas now? How had that happened? And what on earth would they make of the fact that she and Lukas had a child together? A child that she had failed to mention when she had been reunited with them on the day of her father's funeral.

Calista had known this lovely couple for ever, Dorcas had served as a surrogate mother for her during the long hot summers on the island, doing a much better job than her own mother had when she was alive and providing a much-needed pair of loving arms after Diana had died.

They had been the only constant members of staff at Villa Melina. Aristotle's irascible nature had meant that over the years employees would come and go with depressing regularity. And latterly it had been just them, his reduced circumstances meaning that Aristotle hadn't been able to afford any more staff even if he had managed to find any. It occurred to Calista that he probably hadn't even been paying them.

But Thalassa was their home—they had moved here at the same time as Aristotle and Stavros. Calista had worried what would happen to them now that Lukas owned Villa Melina, the island…everything. She wouldn't have been surprised to find he had sacked them on the spot, banished them from Thalassa. He was certainly ruthless enough. But it seemed that not only were they still here on the island, they were working for their former enemy.

She extricated herself from the seatbelt that was wrapped around her and Effie, trying not to wake Effie up as Lukas opened the helicopter door on their side.

'Here—hand her down to me.'

Strong arms reached out to take Effie from her, and reluctantly Calista passed her daughter over before clambering down herself. She noticed the trusting way Effie clung onto her father, nuzzling into him in her sleep as he strode purposefully towards the illuminated villa.

The front door opened and there was Dorcas, silhouetted against the light, her hands clasped to her chest at the sight of Lukas with Effie in his arms.

'Come in, come in—you must all be so tired after your long journey.'

'*Kalispera*, Dorcas.' Calista felt decidedly awkward, embarrassed to be turning up like this with a child no one had known about—not even Aristotle, Effie's grandfather.

But as Dorcas flung her arms around her in the warmest of hugs she felt her anxiety evaporate.

'You are a *bad* girl.' Speaking in English, Dorcas repeatedly kissed her cheeks, clearly delighted. 'You never tell me you have a beautiful daughter. And you and Lukas! Whoever would have thought such a thing?'

Ushering them into the villa, she fussed about, issuing instructions to her husband, who was shaking hands with Lukas, peering curiously at the sleeping bundle in his arms. But when Petros turned to Calista she could see that he too had a broad grin on his face.

'We have made one bedroom into a nursery for little Effie. Petros has painted the walls pink for her—haven't you, Petros?—so that she will love it.'

Petros nodded proudly. But Calista felt an increasing unease. *A nursery?* This was all starting to sound alarmingly permanent.

'Well, thank you, Petros.' Squashing down her fear, Calista reached to take Effie from Lukas's arms. 'If you show me which room it is, I'll put her straight to bed.'

'Of course. Follow me.'

Bustling ahead, Dorcas led the way, opening the door into a room that stopped Calista in her tracks. It had been transformed from what she remembered as a relatively spartan guest room into a pretty nursery, with white-painted furniture, pink and white striped curtains, a child-sized bed, even pictures on the walls of fairies and Disney princesses.

'You like it?' Dorcas whispered expectantly.

'It's lovely, Dorcas. But how did you get it all done so quickly?'

'Lukas say there is no time to waste. It must be done by the time you arrive. So Petros engage a small team of decorators from the mainland. Lukas want everything to be perfect for his daughter.'

Did he indeed?

Her unease was rapidly turning into something more like alarm.

Together she and Dorcas undressed Effie and gently lowered her into the pristine bed, pulling the covers over her and tucking her beloved teddy in beside her. All the time Dorcas was exclaiming in hushed whispers, saying what a beautiful little girl she was, as pretty as her mummy but with her daddy's dark curls. Closing the shutters, Calista almost had to pull her out of the darkened room, leaving the door slightly ajar behind them.

'So are you working *here* now, Dorcas? You and Petros?' Calista was still having trouble figuring this out. She wanted to know what the arrangement was before they re-joined the men.

'Yes. Lukas say he would like us to work for him now.'

'And you are okay with that? I mean after everything that has happened?'

'More than okay, *agapite mou*. Petros and I, we have known Lukas for a very long time, ever since he was a baby. We never believed him to be guilty of such a crime.'

'Really?' Calista stared into the time worn face of kindly woman. 'Then my father... does that mean... did you have suspicions about him, about his involvement?'

'It is not our place to have suspicions, my dear. Now that the Lord has taken the judgement is in His hands.'

Calista swallowed the lump in her throat. 'So, are you living here now? At Villa Helene?'

'No—this is the wonderful thing. Lukas say we can stay at Villa Melina for as long as we want. For ever, even.' The relief was obvious in her voice. 'He say the place is ours.' She turned to look at Calista, suddenly upset. 'I am sorry, Calista—this is your home I talk about. I say to Lukas, *Are you sure you don't want to make Villa Melina your family home?* But he say no—that you will live here, in Villa Helene.'

Now the blood in her veins turned to ice. 'He said *what*, Dorcas? *Who* will live in Villa Helene?'

'All of you—you, Lukas, and dear little Effie, of course. Petros and I couldn't be happier for you. To have a family here on Thalassa again—not just any family, but a Kalanos and a Gianopoulous, joined together like this. Well, it is a dream come true, it really is. To think that Effie will be growing up…'

But Calista could no longer hear Dorcas over the roaring of blood in her ears. A wave of sickness was threatening to knock her legs from under her.

This wasn't just a visit for her and Effie—a few days' stay on Thalassa, even the couple of weeks that Calista had just about been prepared to agree to. Lukas intended that they should stay here *for ever*. No, not *they*—Effie. He had made it quite clear that Calista could do whatever she liked. That she was of no interest to him. It was Effie he wanted. He had as good as kidnapped her.

Well, they would see about that.

Marching back into the living room, Calista squared her shoulders, ready for a fight.

But Lukas met her fierce gaze with infuriating calm. 'Everything all right?'

'No.' Calista spat the word at him. 'Everything is most certainly *not* all right.'

Behind Lukas, Petros was laying the table in front of the window. He looked up with the cutlery in his hand. 'Excuse me? You do not like the room?'

'No—yes. Petros, it's not that. I *love* the room.'

'Your little girl? She no like it?'

'Effie is sound asleep. But I'm sure she will love it when she wakes in the morning.'

'That is good.' Petros went back to laying the table.

'I think what Calista is *trying* to say, Petros, is thank you very much—to you and Dorcas—for doing such a fantastic job in such a short time.'

All relaxed reasonableness, Lukas quirked a dark brow at Calista.

Calista could have hit him—could have cheerfully wiped that smug, supercilious smirk off his face with a hard slap. Except, of course, she had already tried that and it had achieved absolutely nothing. Apart from exposing her lack of control and somehow reinforcing *his* control.

'It was our pleasure, wasn't it, Petros?' Dorcas came bustling through from the kitchen with a casserole dish in her hands. 'Now, come and sit down, both of you. I'm sure you must be very hungry.'

Calista looked from Dorcas to Lukas and back again, suddenly panicky at the idea of being left alone with him. 'Are you and Petros not joining us?'

'Me and Petros? Goodness, no! Whatever are you

thinking, Miss Calista?' Dorcas laughed at her. 'I make this especially for you and Lukas. Your first meal here together as a couple…a family.'

'Thank you, Dorcas. I'm sure it will be delicious.' Lukas interjected smoothly. 'Now, you and Petros must go—you have already done far too much for us. Calista and I will be fine from now on. Won't we, Calista?'

'Fine.' Calista spoke the word through clenched teeth. But the door had hardly closed behind them before she launched into her attack. 'Would you like to tell me what the *hell* is going on?'

Pulling the cork from a bottle of wine, Lukas glanced at her briefly before casually pouring two glasses and handing one to her.

'Going on…?' Now he was serving up the meal—dolloping moussaka onto two plates and placing one before her. 'I wasn't aware that anything was "going on". Please—do sit down.'

Calista thumped into her seat. 'Why do Dorcas and Petros seem to think we will all be living here, as a family? What have you said to them?'

He took a forkful of moussaka, chewing and then swallowing before deigning to reply. 'I suppose Dorcas may have got ahead of herself. She has a rather excitable nature.'

'I'll say she has. You need to put her straight, Lukas. Tell her that Effie and I are only here for a short holiday. That we're returning to the UK.'

'I was actually referring more to our situation—me and you. It would seem that Dorcas has got it into her head that we are a couple. An understandable mistake, I suppose, especially for an old romantic like her.'

'Well, yes—obviously she's got that wrong as well.'

'Aren't you going to eat anything?' Lukas waved at her plate with his fork. 'It's really very good. I can see now how your father got so fat, with Dorcas cooking for him.'

Sticks and stones. Calista refused to rise to the bait.

'So are you going to tell her or shall I? That we're not staying, I mean.'

'You can tell her what you like, Calista. You can *do* what you like. Neither thing is of any interest to me. But Effie will be staying here, with me. For as long as I say.'

'No!'

'Yes, Calista.'

'But that's not what we said. It was to be a short holiday—a fortnight at the most. You agreed.'

'Did I?' Lukas continued to eat his supper, totally unperturbed. 'Perhaps that was a small deception. And don't bother to look so surprised. You are hardly a stranger to deceit yourself.'

'That's not fair!'

'None of this is *fair*, Calista. Having my father die from a heart attack wasn't fair, being thrown into prison for four and a half years wasn't fair, and not being told I have a daughter wasn't fair. But now I intend to redress the balance. From now on things are going to be done *my* way. Starting with Effie staying here on Thalassa with me.'

'No! You can't take your grudge against me and my father out on Effie.'

'I have no intention of taking *anything* out on Effie. Quite the reverse. I look forward to building a relationship with her, being a part of her life.'

'But you can't just *keep* her here!'

'I think you will find that I can. Oh, we can do it the hard way, if you like—lawyers, courts, injunctions— but I would advise against it if I were you. Because I *will* win. I can assure you of that. I'm sure I don't need to remind you that we are on Greek soil and Effie is three-quarters Greek.'

'And *I'm* sure I don't need to remind *you* that you have been in prison for arms-smuggling!'

Calista regretted the words before they had left her mouth. The look of thunderous fury on Lukas's face curdled the contents of her stomach.

'No, Calista.' His voice was a low, mean drawl. 'You do *not* need to remind me. And, believe me, I intend to clear my name. But in the meantime I have money and I have contacts. To try and fight me would be very foolish indeed. I am confident the Greek authorities would look favourably on my custody application.'

'Custody application?' Calista thought she might pass out. 'You intend to fight for *custody* of Effie?'

'Maybe… I'm not sure yet.' Lukas picked up his glass and swilled the wine around. 'That all depends.'

'On what?' She could hear the panic in her voice, strangling her vocal cords.

'On you. On how you behave. If you persist in being

difficult, obstructing me, fighting me every step of the way, then you will leave me no alternative.'

'So what do you expect me to do? Hand over my daughter to you? Agree to all your terms and conditions without question? Roll over and let you do whatever you want?'

'Well…' The air between them suddenly thickened like syrup. 'If you're offering…'

'I am not offering *anything*.'

'No?' A lazy smile curved his lips. 'That's a shame. Because if you were to roll over and let me do whatever I wanted, I guarantee you would enjoy it.'

'Stop this, Lukas.'

'As would I, of course. Because despite everything you've done, despite who you are, I find that I still want you.'

'Well, I don't want *you*.' She threw the words back at him far too fast, and with far too much passion. And they elicited totally the wrong response—a low, primal groan of amusement.

'No? Of course you don't.' His arrogant smirk belied his words.

Calista looked away, refusing to dignify his facetious comment by attempting to challenge it. Besides, there was a danger she would only dig herself a deeper hole.

'So, you see, how we proceed is up to you. You allow Effie to stay here, accept that she has just as much right to be with me as she does with you, and we can keep everything amicable. No court cases, no custody battles—at least for the time being. Just a civilised arrangement between the two of us.'

Calista bit down on her trembling lip. She felt anything *but* civilised. She felt like a wild, raging beast. One that would do anything to protect its young. But she also knew that to try and fight Lukas on this would be extremely dangerous. She had no doubt that he would carry out his threat to take her to court for custody of Effie. And that he would most likely win.

'It seems that I have no choice.' Her heart thumped heavily in her chest.

Lukas shrugged.

'But I'm not leaving Effie here on her own. If she stays, I stay too.'

'As you wish.'

'Very well.' She sucked in a breath. 'I will agree to Effie remaining here, to us both remaining here, at least for the time being. But this is not for ever, Lukas. Effie starts school in September. Obviously we need to be back in the UK by then.'

'I'm very glad that you have decided to see sense.'

Lukas's eyes slowly travelled over her heated face, down her throat and across her chest, lingering on the swell of her breasts beneath the pale blue tee shirt. Instantly Calista felt her nipples harden, and she folded her arms to cover them up. Lukas responded with the quirk of a dark eyebrow.

'And who knows?' he drawled idly. 'Maybe it doesn't have to be so bad. Maybe we can find some interesting ways to keep each other entertained.'

'I am here strictly for Effie. That's all. Do I make myself clear?'

'Crystal-clear. But, unfortunately for you, like crystal I can see right through you.' His lips twitched with a deadly smile. 'And do you know what I see? A woman fighting her sexual desires. A woman who already knows it's a losing battle because deep down she wants me. Much more that she will ever admit.'

'You are *wrong*, Lukas Kalanos. You are nothing but conceited, arrogant and delusional.'

'Am I, indeed?' Lukas put his head on one side, his eyes glittering as dark as the night. 'Well, it takes one to know one.'

Lukas watched his fiery companion through narrowed eyes. She might be fooling herself, he thought complacently, but she wasn't fooling him. Despite the hot-headed rant, her determination to take him to task, the abject denial that he meant anything to her, Calista's body had given her away. And what was more she knew it. The way those rounded breasts had hitched beneath the tight tee shirt, her nipples hardening at his provocative words, had infuriated her as much as it had delighted him.

Lukas had never had any trouble attracting women. The combination of his dark good looks and easy charm had made him a magnet for members of the female sex ever since he'd hit puberty. Even during his time in prison the few women who had worked there had been putty in his hands—the social workers, the prison librarian, the cooks. It had been well known that the Kalanos charm bought special privileges, and rather than complain about it the wiser inmates had kept in with him in the hope of picking up the scraps.

But something about Calista's obvious arousal was special. Maybe it was because of the way she tried to deny it, or because it showed he had some power over her.

Or maybe it was just because it was her.

He had always known that she would never leave Effie alone with him. They came as a pair—that much was obvious. Telling Calista that he didn't care whether she stayed or not had been a bluff he'd been sure of winning. Because he *did* care. He was beginning to realise that he cared too much. He felt a creeping sort of awareness that she was somehow invading his thought processes, influencing his judgement.

It did nothing to improve his temper, and at the same time sent his libido soaring off the scale.

He picked up the wine bottle, gesturing towards Calista's glass but only refilling his own when she shook her head. His eyes travelled to the wall behind them—the scene of their crazed lovemaking session only a couple of days before. No, they hadn't made love—they had had sex. Fast, furious, frantic sex.

At the time he had been too riddled with lust to examine what he was doing, but afterwards he hadn't experienced any of the sense of satisfaction he had expected to feel. Instead he'd been left with a vague feeling of distaste.

Not for Calista, or for what they had done—never that. Far from regretting their coupling it had just made him want more…much more. Far from dulling the hunger that clawed inside him, it had turned it into a dangerously powerful craving. The distaste was for the way he had behaved. His motives, his twisted reasoning…

Lukas took a gulp of wine, searching his brain to try and find some justification for this unwanted attack of conscience. All those years without a woman in his bed was bound to have messed with his head. Especially when he considered the lifestyle he had enjoyed prior to walking into Ms Gianopoulous's trap.

As a young man in his twenties he had enjoyed himself, making the most of his looks, his wealth and his power. He'd loved woman, and women had loved him—as the string of beauties who had graced his bed would be able to testify. He fully intended to pick up where he left off…make up for lost time. But first he had to get this infuriating woman out of his system.

Plus there was the fact that he was now a father. Perhaps bedding a succession of women was no longer appropriate. Perhaps it was time to be more responsible. He certainly wouldn't want his daughter faced with a variety of different lovers over the breakfast table. Not that that had *ever* been his way. He had always preferred the anonymity of a hotel room—valued the freedom of being able to close the door and walk away. He'd believed in keeping his private life private.

Unlike Aristotle, of course.

Lukas looked across at Calista, who was pushing her food around her plate, her cheeks still flaming with resentment. Aristotle had had no qualms about parading his latest conquests around in front of his daughter—or anyone else, for that matter.

That was if you could call the succession of increasingly greedy and desperate women that he'd taken to his bed 'conquests'. The older he'd got, the more obese he'd become—and the more obvious it had been what those women were after. And it certainly hadn't been his body. Or his bonhomie or his grace.

He had never been faithful to any of his three wives. Each marriage had ended in misery or, in the case of Calista's mother, tragedy. And Calista had grown up with that. A different woman in residence every time she returned to Thalassa for the holidays…sometimes more than one. She had witnessed the terrible destruction Aristotle had wreaked on her own mother, ending in her death. And yet still she had been prepared to do his bidding—prepared to debase herself and betray Lukas. Still she had stood by Aristotle's grave with a single lily in her hand, the dutiful daughter to the end.

Frowning, Lukas put down his fork. None of it made any sense to him. Unless, of course, Calista was telling the truth about that fateful night. Unless it really *had* been pure coincidence that she had come to him—not to trap him but because she'd wanted him to make love to her.

No. He refused to be fooled. No doubt the old adage was true—blood was thicker than water. Look at how he felt about Effie. Three days ago he hadn't even known he had a daughter. Now she was already shaping his life, changing his future. There was certainly no way he would allow *her* to be treated the way Aristotle had treated Calista. No way would he let Effie be subjected to such cruel indignity. The very thought of emulating Aristotle Gianopoulous in any way turned his stomach.

Because little Effie had already won his heart.

With a stab of surprise Lukas realised there was nothing, absolutely nothing he wouldn't do for her—to protect her, to keep her safe. He intended to be a very permanent fixture in her life.

The question was, what the hell was he going to do about her mother?

CHAPTER SIX

'WAKE UP, SLEEPYHEAD.'

Calista opened her eyes to see her daughter clambering into bed beside her. She was clutching a half-eaten *koulouri* in her hand—a ring-shaped bread roll, covered in sesame seeds that were now being scattered liberally over the bedclothes.

'You need to get up.'

Calista drew Effie towards her, breathing in her gorgeous little girl smell.

'Good morning, my darling. Did you sleep well?'

'Yes.' Effie squirmed impatiently in her arms. 'But you need to hurry up. We've got a busy day.'

Calista propped herself up on one elbow, pushing the hair out of her eyes. Checking her watch, she was surprised to see how long she had slept—a deep, drugging sort of sleep that had left her brain feeling slow to catch up. But the harsh reality of where she was kicked in soon enough.

She had spent the night in the largest bedroom in the villa, Dorcas having obviously decided to allocate it to the happy couple, filling it with fresh flowers and scented candles. She had even scattered rose petals over the bed—something which had produced a sardonic smile from Lukas when he had opened the door and ushered her in, suggesting she might like to make this room her own before turning to disappear down the corridor. She could still see some of the crumpled petals caught in the bedding.

Now she was faced with the reality of what she had agreed to—staying here on Thalassa with Effie, at least for the foreseeable future. But what choice did she have? She had no money, no contacts. She didn't doubt that Lukas had plenty of both, and the memory of the smug, self-satisfied way he had informed her of that still managed to send her blood pressure skywards.

But then *everything* about Lukas Kalanos sent her blood pressure rocketing skywards. And not just her blood pressure either. Her common sense, her self-control, her temper and her sanity all seemed to cut loose from their moorings when she was around him—not to mention her libido. Just the sight of his lean, muscular body, the athletic way he moved, the tilt of his head or the quirk of his dark brow was enough to see her fighting to hang on to her composure, to counter the extraordinary effect he had on her.

'Come on, Mummy. We are going on my daddy's boat.'

Closing her eyes against an inward groan, Calista opened them again to see her daughter's excited face.

A day on Lukas's boat—that was all she needed. Sailing was Lukas's passion—something he had skilfully turned from an indulgent hobby to an extremely successful business by investing in a fleet of luxury yachts and renting them out. Most of his business was conducted from the mainland, but at any one time there had always been a few of his magnificent, sleek vessels anchored off the coast of Thalassa. As a youngster Calista had loved to watch them glittering in the sunshine, gently rocking on the azure sea.

She had loved to watch Lukas too, who had never been happier than when he was clambering barefoot over the deck of a boat or sailing into the wind, his dark curls blowing madly in the breeze and the spray of the sea on his face. She knew that he preferred sailing the smaller, more intimate yachts in favour of the floating gin palaces—remembered him telling her that it made him feel more at one with the sea, more alive.

'Quickly, Mummy. Get dressed!'

Taking in a deep breath, Calista pushed back the covers and swung her legs over the edge of the bed—but there she stopped. The image of Lukas, smiling and relaxed, his eyes dancing with the exhilaration of a day's hard sailing, had lodged in her mind and refused to be shifted. He had had such a zest for life back then—had been so spirited. So free.

And that freedom had been taken away from him.

She stretched her arms out to her sides to steady herself, bunching the sheets in her hands. For the first time she thought about what it must have been like for him—*really* thought. For Lukas, of all people, to have been deprived of the outside world, the sun and the sea, the rolling waves and the whistling wind. To lose his freedom for four and a half years…

It must have been torture for him—pure torture. Which would have been bad enough if he'd been guilty. But what if he *had* been wrongly convicted? What if all this time he had been innocent...?

Calista put her fist in her mouth, biting down on her knuckles. Ever since her world had exploded so dramatically she had been using Lukas's 'crime' as a shield to protect herself, to keep her strong. She couldn't help it that she had fallen in love with him. Fallen into a deeply painful, fathomless love that could never be cured. But Lukas was not the man she'd thought he was. He had been convicted of a heinous offence, as an accomplice in a shockingly immoral crime.

Finding out she was pregnant with his child might have all but finished her—felled her on the spot—especially as she had been so young, so alone. But it hadn't. She had pulled through—more than pulled though. She had done a great job of raising her daughter single-handedly, as well as completing her nursing training and making sure there was always enough money to keep them both fed and clothed. Somehow she had drawn strength from Lukas's disgrace. From the knowledge that she was on her own. That she was totally responsible for both her own life and her daughter's.

And during her darkest hours—those miserable lonely nights when she had thought the dawn would never come—she had forced herself to remember what Lukas had done, the man he really was. Used his terrible crime as a prop to keep her upright.

But now that prop had gone—had been kicked away

from under her. Now she was left sprawling on the floor by the shockingly painful truth. *Lukas was innocent.* She knew it in her heart—maybe she had always known it.

Which meant that her own father had been as guilty as sin.

'Mummy!' Effie slipped her hand into hers, attempting to tug her to her feet. 'Daddy is waiting for us.'

Heading to the bathroom, Calista felt as if her legs were made of lead. She would have to talk to Lukas— face up to the truth, no matter how painful it was. If nothing else, she owed him that.

Shading her eyes from the glare of the sun, Calista watched her daughter splashing about in the turquoise sea. Effie and Lukas were some distance from the boat, but instinctively Calista trusted Lukas to keep her safe. Effie couldn't yet swim—it was one of the things Calista had been meaning to teach her, but the thought of London's municipal swimming pools hadn't held much appeal. Now a couple of brightly coloured water wings were keeping her afloat as Lukas patiently explained to her how to kick her legs, holding her under the tummy and getting showered in the process.

'Well done—nearly there.' His voice carried clearly across the water. 'Now, see if you can swim across to me.'

Taking a few strokes away, he turned and waited for her to splash towards him, her little legs kicking wildly behind her.

'Yay, you did it!' Catching her up in his arms, he

held her aloft to squeals of merriment, before safely tucking her beside him to swim back to the boat.

Calista quickly returned to her book.

'Did you see that, Mummy?'

The boat started to rock as first Effie and then Lukas climbed aboard.

'I was swimming all by myself.'

'That's brilliant, darling.' Calista made a show of closing her book and putting it down beside her, to prove that she was now in charge. She rose to her feet. 'Now, come on—let's get you dry.'

Moving in for a hug, Effie pressed her chilly wet body against Calista's sun-warmed skin, sending a rash of goosebumps skittering all over her. She felt Lukas's merciless gaze travelling over every bare inch of her. Concentrating on pulling the water wings off Effie's skinny arms, she took hold of her hand and made her way towards the cabin.

But Lukas was in the way.

'Excuse me.' She tried to squeeze past him but still he refused to move, meaning she had no alternative but to raise her eyes to the magnificence of his body, to take in all his masculine glory. Just as he had planned she would.

Wearing an extremely snug pair of black trunks that left little to the imagination, he stood before her, the epitome of glorious manhood, tall and bronzed, with sculpted muscles in all the right places. Droplets of water glittered on his skin and in his tightly curled chest hair, running in rivulets down his long, shapely legs and pooling at his feet on the varnished wood of the deck.

Calista swallowed. She had already sneaked a look at him when he had taken a graceful dive into the sea, before swimming round to the steps at the back of the boat to help Effie into the water. That had been more than enough to get her pulse racing. This blatant display of rampant masculinity was in danger of sending it into overdrive.

Mustering what little will-power she had left, she stepped deliberately round him, chin in the air, and led Effie down into the relative cool of the cabin.

'Next time I'm going to do it without the water wings.' Teeth chattering, Effie let herself be towelled dry. 'Daddy says I'm a fast learner.'

'I'm sure you are.' Rubbing at the dark curls, Calista kissed her daughter lightly on the nose. 'But you don't have to call him Daddy, you know. Not if you don't want to…not if it seems too soon. It's quite all right to call him Lukas.

'That's okay, I like calling him Daddy. He says that the Greek children call their daddies Bampas. That's funny, isn't it?' She wrinkled her little nose happily. 'Is that what you called *your* daddy?'

No, Calista thought silently. She had never called Aristotle anything other than the formal word—Pateras. The more affectionate Bampas had seemed wrong when addressing the short-tempered, irascible, rather frightening figure that her father had been.

'And the word for yes is *nai*.' Effie was still chattering on as Calista tugged dry clothes onto her. 'That's funny too. Daddy said I must learn how to speak *all* the Greek words—then I can talk to anyone.'

'Well, we'll see.' Calista tried to disguise the tension in her voice. 'You won't need to speak Greek when we go back to London, will you?'

'S'pose not. I like it *here*, though.' Giving a yawn, Effie twisted a damp curl around her finger.

'Yes. Holidays are fun, aren't they?' Calista persisted. 'But going home will be good too. I bet Magda is missing us.'

'Hmm...' Effie nodded thoughtfully. 'P'raps she could come here too?'

'No, I don't think so darling. Now, d'you want to have a little nap?'

To her surprise Effie nodded and, lifting her arms, let Calista carry her through to one of the cabins, where she gently laid her down on the bed. Her eyes closed almost immediately.

Calista looked around her, tempted to stay down there rather than go back on deck and have to face Lukas again. But that would be cowardly—and she was not a coward. Reluctantly she climbed up into the sunshine.

Lukas had his back to her, squatting on the bow of the boat, doing something with some ropes.

Hearing her approach he turned. 'Effie okay?'

'Yes, she's fine. She's having a sleep. Must be all this fresh air.' She attempted a light-hearted laugh.

'A child can never have too much fresh air.'

Calista pursed her lips. So he was the expert now, was he? She watched with feigned indifference as he lithely rose to his feet and came towards her.

'Can I get you anything?' He bent to open the cool box that held the remains of their picnic. 'More food? A beer?'

'No, thanks.' She was already regretting the glass of chilled white wine she had had earlier. What with that and the sun, her head was starting to swim a little. 'I think I'll just sit under the canopy here and read my book.'

'As you wish.'

Arranging herself on the comfortable cushions in the shade, Calista opened her novel. She heard the hiss of gas as Lukas took the cap off a bottle of beer, and raised her eyes to see him moving about with the bottle in one hand, checking on the winches of the rolled up sails, swinging under the beam to get to the back of the boat. The sea slapped gently on the sides. A seagull squawked overhead. She closed her eyes...

Lukas eased his tall frame onto the cushions beside Calista. She was sleeping peacefully, and a strand of red hair was caught on her slightly open lips, moving as she breathed. He let his eyes travel slowly over her body, lingering on the swell of her breasts under the small emerald-green triangles of her bikini top. Two strips of bare skin were just visible beneath, peeking out from where she had shifted and dislodged the fit of the bikini.

Lukas's throat moved. The temptation to run his finger over the exposed pale flesh was almost too much to resist. Or to run his tongue over it...then release the string ties around her neck and push the fabric away, so that his mouth could give her warm, full breasts the attention that they so blatantly deserved… He felt himself harden painfully beneath his trunks.

Tearing his eyes away, he looked out to sea to the hazy horizon way in the distance. He knew if he put his mind to it he could have pretty much any woman he wanted. So why was he torturing himself by lusting after this one? How had Calista got to him like this, so that his whole body thrummed for her…ached for her? Why was it that suddenly no other woman held the slightest interest for him?

He had been her first lover, of course. Could that explain this ludicrous obsession? He would never forget the moment they had both realised that there was no going back. That first exquisite moment of penetration when Calista had gasped for air, holding herself rigid as he had eased himself so carefully into her. The way she had clung to him, urging him in further, deeper, until she had taken all of him.

She had been so passionate, so aroused, so totally convincing. Over the years he had told himself that it must have been an act. But now… Now he wasn't so sure. Now when he looked into those remarkable green eyes of hers he saw lots of things—anger, hurt, fear, defiance. But not betrayal. And when he had laid bare Aristotle's guilt before her she had looked genuinely devastated. Broken.

Lukas raked a hand through his damp hair, narrowing his eyes as he watched the white sails of the boats in the distance. He wanted to move on, to stop agonising over the past and concentrate on the future. A future that would now most definitely involve his daughter.

Because Effie was the one truly miraculous thing to have come out of this mess. He still found it hard to believe that he had fathered a daughter. And one as undoubtedly special as Effie. He got a buzz every time he looked at her…every time he thought about her.

But there was something far less agreeable he was struggling to come to terms with. Something that had grown from an annoying niggle into a monster that refused to go away. He might have been Calista's first partner, but how many lovers had she had since? Five years had passed—ample time for her to have taken up with any number of suitors.

The very thought of her with another man—any man—boiled the blood in his veins, made his hands shake with impotent fury.

At least there didn't appear to be anyone on the scene at the moment. He'd had a quiet word with Effie, casually mentioning Mummy and her boyfriend in the same sentence, and had been mightily relieved when she had just looked at him in puzzlement.

That didn't mean there wasn't someone in the background, of course, but the way Calista had given herself to him on the day of the funeral—with such need, such greed, even, like a starving woman—suggested that there wasn't. Or if there had been he was now history. Or he damned soon would be. Because Calista was going to be his and his alone for as long as he deemed fit. To do with as he deemed fit.

Had he always intended this? Lukas wasn't sure.

But the decision was made now. He wanted Calista. Not just once—clearly that had done nothing to slake his thirst—and not even for the occasional casual sex, albeit amazing. He wanted her in his bed every single night. And, more than that, he was going to make sure that she wanted *him*.

Hearing her stir, he turned back to look at her, watching as she moistened her lips with the tip of her tongue, moved back against the cushions. Leaning forward, he picked up the book that was resting on her stomach, the open pages sticking slightly to the suntan lotion on her skin. He had watched her applying it earlier on, rubbing it onto shoulders dusted with freckles, then her chest, down her arms and the flat of her stomach. He had been itching to take over, to smooth the lotion over her himself, to push aside the scraps of fabric and let his hot fingers slide across her breasts, her buttocks, to the places that were hidden from the sun...

But too late—or maybe just in time—she had finished. Snapping the cap of the bottle shut and shooting him a look of such haughty disdain it had made him smile despite himself.

Now she opened sleepy green eyes. He was close enough to see a split-second swirl of desire before alarm and then indignation took over.

'Lukas!' She scrabbled to push herself upright, sweeping her hair away from her face. 'You made me jump.'

'Guilty conscience?'

'No.' Immediately she was on the defensive. 'What are you doing, anyway? Why are you watching me?'

'Just admiring the view.'
'Well, don't.'

Calista didn't know which Lukas she found the more intimidating—the fiercely brutal and vengeful one she had been met with at her father's funeral, or the arrogantly sarcastic one who was deliberately letting his gaze rake over her now.

Neither of them represented the Lukas she had once known. The one she had fallen in love with. And yet she *had* caught a glimpse of that man. She had seen it in the way he was with Effie—so gentle, so patient. She had even seen it earlier on today, when he had been at the helm of the yacht, shooting her an unexpected smile as they had tacked fast into the wind, the pleasure of doing something he so clearly loved making him forget himself for a minute. Forget how much he hated her.

Calista felt her body begin to tingle beneath his scrutiny, the thrum of desire starting its traitorous beat. She needed to put a stop to it.

'Is there any water in the cool box?'

'Sure.'

Pushing himself to stand with one lithe movement, Lukas retrieved a bottle of mineral water and passed it to her. Calista took several deep gulps and looked down at herself. Even in the shade her skin was starting to turn pink—she burnt so easily it was ridiculous. She was glad that Effie wasn't going to have the same problem. She had inherited her father's colouring, albeit several shades lighter.

Feeling restored by the water, she started to get to her feet. 'I'm just going to check on Effie.'

'No need. I just did. She's still asleep.'

'Oh, right.' Calista sat back down.

There had been a cold inflexibility in Lukas's voice—as if he expected her to challenge him, or as if he was waiting for something. His eyes held hers for a couple of seconds before he stretched himself out on the cushions beside her, lying on his side with one arm under his head to prop him up.

He looked magnificent, even from the quick sideways glance that was all she would allow herself. She refused to give him the satisfaction of ogling that beautiful body, those tanned, honed muscles that screamed to be admired, to be touched. Because that was what he wanted. For some reason he seemed determined to taunt her with his perfect physique.

Calista pulled up her knees and hugged them to her chest. The more blatant his display, the more she was determined to cover herself up.

A couple of highly charged seconds ticked by, Lukas owned the silence by doing absolutely nothing. Calista drew in a breath. There was one sure way to counter the sexual tension that he was deliberately stoking between them. Much as she hated to fling herself into the pit of misery that had been caused by her father, she knew that she had to.

She cleared her throat. 'Lukas, I've been thinking.'

She shifted nervously on the sun lounger, forcing herself to meet his gaze. Lukas quirked a dark brow in response.

'What you were saying about my father…it's true, isn't it? He *was* responsible for the arms-smuggling.'

'Yes, Calista. It's true.' He stared at her, scanning her face with an intensity that stripped her bare—as if he could read her mind, see her more clearly than she could see herself.

'And Stavros, he had no part in it, did he?'

'None whatsoever.'

'And neither did you.'

With a very slight tilt of the head, his reply was given in the glittering blackness of his eyes.

An agonising second ticked by. The yacht rocked gently from the wake of a fishing boat heading out to sea. Calista wished that she was on it. That she could leap aboard and be chugged further and further away from this awful situation.

Instead she wrapped her arms around her knees more tightly, letting her hair fall over her face to cover her shame as she stared down at her painted toenails.

'I'm so sorry, Lukas.' It came out as barely more than a whisper.

'Sorry?' Lukas repeated the word, rolling it around his mouth as if it were made of stone. 'I hardly think "sorry" makes up for what happened.'

'Well, no, but…'

'Makes up for taking away my freedom, blackening my name, ruining my life.'

'No. I mean obviously nothing will make up for that.'

'For killing my father.'

That brought Calista's head up.

'That's not fair.' She lifted her hair from the nape of

her neck to try and cool herself down. 'Stavros had a weak heart—it said so in the autopsy report. He could have died at any time.'

'And yet he died after a furious row with Aristotle.'

'Even so...'

'Still defending him, Calista? That monster of a father of yours?'

'No—'

'Because if so I suggest you open your eyes and take a long, hard look at the man who sired you.'

'I don't want to. I don't need to.'

'Because if you did you would see exactly the sort of vile creature he was.'

'I know he did a terrible thing, Lukas.'

Close to tears, Calista covered her face with shaking hands. Admitting her father's guilt was excruciatingly painful but she knew she had to face up to it before she could move on. Face up to Lukas too, who shimmered quietly beside her like some sculpted bronze Greek god. But she wasn't responsible for Aristotle's crime. Despite what Lukas thought, *she* had done nothing wrong. She had to make him see that.

Taking a deep breath, she removed her hands from her face to see Lukas staring at her, his expression inscrutable. 'I swear to you, I had no idea what he was involved in. You *have* to believe me.'

'Okay.' There was a beat of silence before Lukas gave a small shrug. 'I believe you.'

'Good.' Calista felt her shoulders drop. 'Then you accept that I played no part in the conspiracy?'

'If you say so.'

'I do.' On a firmer footing now, Calista straightened up, pushing back her shoulders. This was the point when some sort of small apology from him might be called for. Clearly that wasn't happening. 'Much as I regret what happened, I am not guilty of my father's crimes.'

'No.'

Lukas lifted the arm that was resting over his waist. For a moment Calista thought he was going to touch her, make some sort of conciliatory gesture, but instead he rubbed his hand around the back of his neck.

'But you are still guilty of betraying me.'

'No, I've told you—'

Lukas raised his hand to silence her.

'You accepted your father's version of events without question. You were prepared to believe that I was capable of such a heinous crime without even speaking to me. *That's* the betrayal I'm talking about.'

'I was wrong—I know that now.' She bit down on her lip. 'I'm so sorry I didn't trust you.'

'I don't want your wretched apologies!' Suddenly his voice was harsh, bitter. 'I don't give a damn what you think about me now.' He shifted the length of his body fractionally, his eyes boring into her. 'You still don't get it, do you?'

Calista stared back at him.

'Your father may have been responsible for getting me locked up, but in believing his lies you denied me the knowledge that I was a father. You stole from me the first four and a half years of Effie's life.'

He shook his head in disgust. 'And if we hadn't met at the funeral—if I hadn't dragged it out of you—I still wouldn't know of her existence.'

'No, I *would* have told you. I was *going* to tell you.'

'Really? When, exactly? When she was eighteen? Twenty-one?'

'I had to think of Effie. To put her first…do what was best for her.'

'And what was "best for her" was to deprive her of her father?' His voice leached scorn. 'Thanks for that, Calista.'

Calsita cast about, desperately looking for a way to counter his contempt. 'For your information, life these past few years hasn't exactly been easy for me, you know.'

'Is that so?' He stared at her with obvious distaste. 'Have *you* been sharing a cell with an armed robber who would slit your throat for an ounce of tobacco?'

'Well, no, but…'

'Spent the one hour a day that you're allowed outside marching round a prison courtyard? Had your every movement recorded by security cameras?'

'No, of course I haven't.'

'Then don't you *dare* start telling me you have had it tough.'

'I can't undo the past, Lukas!' she cried out, her voice heavy with the weight of shame. 'I don't know what else I can say.'

'Nothing—there is *nothing* you can say.' There was a long beat of silence. 'But maybe there is something you can *do*.'

Reaching forward, he trailed a finger along her jaw-line, running it over her lips.

Calista felt her heart stutter, her eyes widening as his head lowered until his mouth was barely a centimetre from her own, his breath a whisper of soft promise.

'Maybe there is a way you can start making it up to me...'

And with one lithe movement he swung his magnificent body over hers.

CHAPTER SEVEN

HIS BODY HOVERED above her, braced by locked arms and toes that were pushed firmly into the padded lounger. Calista held herself very still, achingly aware of the corded muscles of his biceps, the hard-packed torso that was only inches away from her trembling body. She could feel the heat radiating off him, prickling over her, finding its way unerringly to her inner core. His breath fanned over her face, making her eyelashes flutter close until his lips touched hers and the familiar bolt of electricity made them shoot open again. One touch—that was all it took. One graze of his lips for her to shake with need. For her to fall apart.

Bending his elbows, Lukas lowered his body, adjusting the angle of his head very slightly until he deemed it just right and increased the pressure of his lips. It was a coaxing, persuasive kiss, gloriously sensual but leaving her in no doubt as to who was in control here—who had all the power.

For a split second Calista tried to fight against it, holding her facial muscles taut, her lips tight. But it was hopeless—and they both knew it. With a giddy rush of surrender she parted her mouth and immediately Lukas was there, giving a low growl of approval as his tongue found hers, tangling and stroking, hot and hard and heavy as he devoured her, stoking the familiar madness that gripped them both.

Calista thrust her hands into his hair, spreading her fingers so that she could hold him to her, seal them together. Sliding one arm under her back, Lukas flipped them so that she was on top of him, their mouths still fused by that burning, bruising kiss. The skin of their near naked bodies was erotically scaled all the way down—and then Lukas peeled them apart, his hand spanning her hips and moving her down until he had her where he wanted her: pressed firmly into his groin, where the length of his arousal welcomed her with its might and its power and its mind-numbing promise.

Calista heard herself moan, the wondrous feel of him shooting through every cell of her body, making her want him inside her so badly she had to stop herself from begging for it, right there and then. Instead she rocked against him, increasing the pressure, heightening the gloriously erotic sensation.

Lukas growled his approval.

The thin fabric of their swimwear was in danger of melding to their skin with the blistering heat they were generating. Raising herself up on one arm, Calista slid a hand between them, running it down the rippling muscles of his chest until she found the straining fabric of Lukas's trunks, where she traced the steel length of him. Lukas gave a primal shudder and suddenly his hands were all over her, pulling at the ties of her bikini behind her back and around her hips, the scraps of fabric falling apart in his hurry to possess her, his animal craving every bit as desperate as her own.

'God, Calista...' He ground the words into her shoulder. 'Look what you do to me.'

His mouth was on hers again, his hands skimming over the warm skin of her naked buttocks, dipping into the valley between, his fingers sliding down to where she wanted him most.

'I can't get enough of you.' He groaned through the kiss. 'I will *never* get enough of you.'

Was that a threat or a promise? Calista didn't know— she didn't care. Her only conscious thought was that she wanted him so badly she feared she might explode with it.

But they had to find some control. Effie was asleep in the cabin below. They had to act responsibly.

As if Calista had somehow willed it to happen they both heard the sound at the same time. A sort of scuffling noise beneath them and then a clear little voice calling out.

'Mummeee!'

Hurriedly pushing herself away from Lukas's body, Calista looked down at herself—at the bikini top that hung loose around her neck, the bottoms that were just a scrap of fabric between her legs.

'I'm coming, darling. Just hang on one minute.'

After fumbling to retie all the fiddly strings she hastily adjusted the triangles of her bikini top to cover nipples stiff with longing, breasts still heavy with desire. Only then did she raise her eyes to Lukas, to see that he had been watching her every move. She caught the intensely dark gleam in his eyes—almost fierce, but with a hint of vulnerability—before he moved away, searching for a pair of board shorts to cover his considerable arousal.

And only just in time. A second later a tousled-haired head appeared at the top of the cabin steps, blinking into the sunshine.

'Here you are.' Effie looked curiously from one to the other, as if they were both being quietly assessed and found to be guilty. 'I didn't know where I was when I woke up.'

'Didn't you, darling?' Calista went to give her daughter a hug. 'It's okay. We're still on the boat.'

'I know that *now*!' She rolled her eyes before a broad grin spread across her pretty face. 'Can I go swimming again?'

'Um…yes, I don't see why not. I think I'll go in with you this time.' The idea of cooling water was suddenly very appealing.

'Yay! And Daddy too?'

'Maybe in a bit.' Lukas moved so that he was standing behind Calista, laying a hand on her shoulder and dipping his head so that he could whisper in her ear. 'To be continued, Ms Gianopoulous.' His breath fanned softly against her hair.

Calista swallowed. But with Effie tugging on her hand she was mercifully spared having to come up with any sort of reply.

* * *

Leaning back in his chair, Lukas stretched his arms behind his head. He had been working in his office all afternoon and he needed a break, but picking up the reins after being away for so long meant a lot of hard work and commitment.

His luxury yachting business, Blue Sky Charters, had been ticking over nicely in his absence. His staff had stayed loyal to him and, even though it hadn't grown the way it would have done had he been there in person to oversee it, it was a very thriving concern. He had been lucky, he supposed—though 'lucky' was hardly a word he would use—that the authorities had made no claim on his personal business. There was no connection between that and G&K Shipping, which had been decimated by the scandal.

But Lukas fully intended to see *that* concern succeed again too, in honour of his father. He had already managed to buy back seven super-tankers. Nothing like the fleet of eighty they had had before Aristotle Gianapoulous had seen fit to blow the business sky-high, but it was a start. He also intended to clear his name—and, far more importantly, his father's name. He wanted the world to know just who had really been responsible for the vile trade in arms. Who the *real* guilty party had been.

Leaning forward, he closed the lid of his laptop. The villa was very quiet and still in the early evening sunshine. Too quiet, he realised. It was over a week since the three of them had arrived at Villa Helene, and Lukas had become used to having Calista and Effie around—to hearing the patter of Effie's feet running along the marble-tiled floors, her shrill little laugh echoing through the open-plan rooms. Even when he should have been relishing his solitude he found himself listening out for them. Just as he was doing now— waiting for sounds to indicate that they had returned from their trip to the beach.

Calista had stuck her head around the door after lunch, to announce that she was taking Effie down to the small sandy cove that was only a few hundred yards from the villa, approached by some rickety old wooden steps. By the tone of her voice it had been quite plain that he wasn't invited. Not that that would have stopped Lukas if he'd wanted to join them, but he had work to do. Besides, it appeared he and Calista were playing some sort of game. Over the past week she had seemed determined to hold him at arm's length, going out of her way to put distance between them whenever she could and finding excuses never to let them be alone together for any length of time.

Lukas had deliberately gone along with it, refusing to react. Being unreasonably reasonable just to wind her up. He'd decided he was prepared to play the long game. Well, long*ish*. In point of fact, watching that pertly rebellious body moving around the villa was driving him crazy—killing him. But in a perverse sort of way he was enjoying it. And knowing with increasing certainty that she was faking her casual indifference only added to the sexual tension that hummed steadily between them.

Lukas looked at his watch. Gone six o'clock. He had

thought they would be back by now—although he knew that Effie always pleaded to stay longer when she was told it was time to leave the beach.

Seeing how much Effie obviously adored being here on Thalassa was a source of great satisfaction to Lukas—not least because of the way it made her mother squirm. On the one hand Calista was obviously happy that her daughter was having such a great time, but she also felt she had to keep reminding her—and him—that this was nothing more than a holiday, that they would shortly be returning to London.

Well, they would see about that. Lukas hadn't fully formulated his plans yet, but when he had he would be making quite sure that Calista abided by them. One thing was certain: now he had discovered Effie he had no intention of letting her go again.

Because he adored everything about this little girl. She had stolen his heart from the very first moment he had laid eyes on her, back in the kitchen of Calista's flat. She was a complete delight—the most unexpected joy to have come out of such terrible circumstances. Lukas would do anything to keep her close. And that included taming her flame haired mother.

Although 'taming' wasn't the right word. Lukas didn't want Calista tamed. He loved that wild, fiery streak of hers. The green eyes that flashed with fire as she glared at him, the way her hair whipped around her face, the nostrils that flared with contempt and the obstinate defiance that held her chin high. She was as maddening as hell, but somehow he kept coming back for more punishment.

And it *did* feel like punishment, the way she had got to him. Like a burr against his skin, she was impossible to ignore, to dismiss. For the sake of his own sanity Lukas had decided he would concentrate only on the sexual attraction between them. That was more understandable. And infinitely more pleasurable.

He would concentrate on the free spirit behind that feisty façade, the vibration between them whenever he took her in his arms, the abandoned, almost feral way she responded. As if overtaken by the force of nature. As if there was nothing she wouldn't do for him or let him do for her. That was what he would focus on. Because Lukas had never experienced a high like it before. No other sexual experience had come even close.

Not that he had been able to put his erotic theories into practice—not yet. They had only made love twice, with a four-and-a-half-year gap in between, and neither time had been perfect. The first time—thrilling though it had been—he had been too shocked, too caught up in the preciousness of the moment to make it last the way he should have. And the second time... Pushing Calista up against the wall and taking her like that had hardly been his finest hour—far from it. No matter how she had responded...how good it had felt.

No, the next time he and Calista made love—because there *was* going to be a next time, and soon—he was going to make sure the conditions were just right. He was going to see just what he and Calista could do together, just what intense sexual magic they were capable of.

Which was why he had spent some time carefully formulating a plan.

This morning a small batch of post had arrived for Calista—presumably forwarded on by the woman she shared her flat with. Petros had picked it up from the mainland and delivered it to the villa, along with a large flaxen-haired doll in a presentation box that he had proudly given to Effie as a gift from him and Dorcas. Effie had thanked him most politely, even though Lukas had seen her looking at it slightly askance. After he had gone she had set about divesting the doll of her fussy dress whilst Lukas had watched Calista flicking through the letters, only bothering to open one, reading it quickly and then stuffing it back in the envelope.

'Anything interesting?' Something about the pinched look on her face had begged the question.

'Not really.' Calista had taken a sip of her coffee. 'It's from my father's lawyer. They're reading the will on the twenty-eighth.'

'As in tomorrow?'

Looking at her phone, she'd checked the date. 'Um… yes.'

'Will you be going?'

'No. The office is in Athens. Besides, I want nothing to do with my father's legacy—not now I know the truth.'

Lukas had watched as she lowered her eyes, picking nervously at the corner of the embossed envelope. It had surprised him that he felt no sense of satisfaction that she had finally accepted the truth. Instead her obvious pain had arrowed to his heart.

'My half-brothers can share whatever meagre spoils there may be between them.'

'Not without you being there to sign them over, they can't.' Lukas had briskly switched to business mode. 'I suggest you go to Athens and take this opportunity to legally tie up the loose ends. Then perhaps you can move on.'

'And *I* suggest you drop the amateur psychology and mind your own business.'

Lukas had waited for the anger to kick in. Normally he didn't take kindly to being spoken to like that. Normally he would have made the perpetrator pay. But Calista's backlash had simply served to show him she still had plenty of fight left in her. It was almost a relief.

'Touched a nerve, have I?'

'No. I just don't need you to tell me what I should and shouldn't be doing, thank you very much.'

'Very well. But perhaps you might allow me to make a small suggestion. I also have business in Athens. We could go there tomorrow...maybe stay overnight in my apartment.'

'No,' Calista had replied firmly. 'It would be too disruptive for Effie.'

'Then perhaps Effie could stay here?' He had kept his voice deliberately light. 'I'm sure Dorcas and Petros would be happy to look after her.'

'Oh, *please*, Mummy.' Never one to miss a trick, Effie had looked up from where she had been walking the semi-clad doll across the table, turning her big green eyes on her mother. 'Can I stay with Dorcas and Petros? *Please?*'

'I don't know...' Calista had hurried to find an excuse. 'I mean, they might not want the bother of looking after you overnight.'

'Oh, they will. And, anyway, I won't be any bother. I can help Dorcas make some *kouloulou* biscuits.'

'Koulourakia,' Calista had prompted, repeating the name of the buttery biscuits that Effie loved so much.

'Yes, those. So *can* I, Mummy?'

'Well, maybe. We'll talk about it later.'

At which point Lukas had allowed himself a secret smile. Thanks to his brilliantly wonderful daughter, step one of his plan had been successfully implemented.

Now he walked through the empty villa and out onto the terrace, shading his eyes against the glare of the swimming pool. In the distance he could hear the faint chatter of a small voice, coming closer, and then mother and daughter appeared at the top of the steps to his left. They both looked warm and windswept. Calista was wearing a sarong tied low around her hips and was weighed down by a beach bag and a cool box. Effie was struggling with an inflatable crocodile that was nearly twice her size, the breeze flapping it against her small body.

As Lukas started towards them he realised with a jolt of surprise just how pleased he was to see them.

'What the hell is *he* doing here?'

Calista's two half-brothers jumped to their feet as she and Lukas entered the lawyer's office. Behind her, Calista felt Lukas stiffen.

'He has no business being here.' Christos directed his venom at her. 'Get him out, Calista.'

'Sit down, Christos.' With a calm she didn't feel, Calista took a seat across the desk from the aged lawyer. 'Lukas is merely accompanying me.'

'To survey the damage he has caused, most likely.' Christos's eyes bulged in his head. 'To check that he has decimated our inheritance as much as he has his own. The cheating, lousy, lowlife—'

'Why would you want him here, Calista?' Yiannis cut across his brother when the sound of Lukas's intake of breath was enough tell him that Christos was in danger of getting himself into serious trouble.

Calista hadn't actually wanted Lukas to join them, but somehow she had ended up being cleverly outmanoeuvred by him. First he had insisted on delivering her to the revolving door of the office block, then on accompanying her in the lift to the correct floor, and before she had known it he had followed her right in.

'Why don't we all sit down?' From the other side of the desk Mr Petrides, the Gianopoulous family lawyer, who had to be at least eighty years old, showed that he had no time for family squabbles. 'The reading of the will shouldn't take too long. For Calista's benefit I will speak in English, if that is agreeable to you all?'

'Just get on with it.'

Christos returned to his seat, followed by Yiannis. Lukas drew up a chair to sit on the other side of Calista.

Clearing his throat, Mr Petrides began slowly reading through the legal jargon. Calista tried to concentrate, but it was difficult with Lukas beside her, sitting perfectly still but radiating enough suppressed hostility towards the Gianopoulous brothers to decimate a small country. Was he planning some sort of showdown? Was that why he was here? For the first time she wondered if she had been tricked into bringing them all together. But if so, did it matter?

Time ticked by. The office was cramped and stuffy, and before long Calista found her mind wandering. She hoped Effie was okay, although she didn't really have any doubt that she would be. Dorcas and Petros had been absolutely delighted by the idea of babysitting for twenty-four hours, and all three had waved them off gleefully. The couple were staying overnight at Villa Helene—presumably Lukas still didn't want his daughter anywhere near Aristotle's Villa Melina.

She, of course, had somehow found herself agreeing to stay the night at Lukas's Athens apartment. She had never been there before. As a teenager she had tried not to think about it, imagining all the women Lukas might have taken back there, picturing some sort of wild bachelor pad with black satin sheets and handcuffs hanging off the bedhead. Not that Lukas had ever given her reason to think that. He had been notoriously discreet about his private life. But that didn't mean he hadn't had one.

One thing was for sure: tonight she was going to have to be careful not to slip between those black satin sheets herself. All week long, ever since *that* kiss on the boat, she had been fighting the crippling effect he had on her. The seductive power that made her speech stilted, made her steps stumbling, made her insides turn to jelly.

So she had deliberately distanced herself from him, avoiding potentially intimate situations by ensuring that Effie was with her at all times. And in the evenings, after she'd had no alternative but to put Effie to bed, by burying her head in a book or deciding on an early night.

And, surprisingly, Lukas had put no pressure on her at all. In fact he had behaved like the perfect gentleman. Far from trying to persuade her to stay for a nightcap on the terrace, or go for a stroll under the starlit sky, he had seemed perfectly happy to see her disappear, politely wishing her goodnight before returning to his laptop and burying himself in work.

Calista had told herself that was a relief. He had obviously forgotten his whispered promise on the boat. He had decided to drop the whole seduction routine and give her some space. But as the days had gone on somehow her relief had turned to frustration and then doubt. His gentlemanly conduct had started to seem more like uninterest than respect. And despite herself Calista had found that she was lingering a few seconds longer than strictly necessary when she said goodnight, holding his dark hooded gaze when she should have looked away, threading her fingers through her hair in what might have been construed as a suggestive manner.

Not that it had made any difference. In return Lukas had simply given her one of his infuriating half-smiles, leaving her feeling flustered and stupid before heading for the safety of her room.

'So basically you are telling us that there is absolutely *nothing*!'

Christos's furious voice jolted her back to the present.

Mr Petrides surveyed him over the top of his glasses. 'I am saying that the small amount of assets your father had will need to be divided between his remaining creditors.'

'And Thalassa?' Yiannis leant forward. 'That has gone too?'

'There is no mention of the island of Thalassa.' Mr Petrides looked down at the papers before him. 'My understanding is that it was the property of your father's first wife and has recently been sold. To Mr Kalanos.'

'Why, you—'

Christos was on his feet again, but Yiannis intercepted, roughly shoving him back in his seat.

'So it is true?' Yiannis turned to Lukas, defeat etched into his face.

'Just as I said,' Lukas replied with icy calm, his fingers steepled beneath his chin, his gaze steady.

'So why the hell are we here?' Christos turned on Mr Petrides. 'Just to be humiliated? So that this man can gloat over the despicable way he has tricked us?'

'No, Christos.' The old man suddenly seemed to age before their eyes. 'The reason I have gathered you here today is because I have something to tell you. I believe it is time you learned the truth about your father.' He sat back, a shudder racking his body. 'These past few years I have kept quiet. At the time I thought it was out of loyalty to your father, but now I see it was just cowardice. However, now the situation has changed. I have been diagnosed with a terminal illness. And I feel the need to unburden myself before I die.'

'Oh, I am *so* sorry, Mr Petrides.' Calista reached forward to take hold of his hand, but he withdrew it, placing it in his lap.

'I don't deserve your sympathy, Calista. You see, I have been concealing information—from you and from the police. I am very sorry to have to tell you this…' He cast rheumy eyes over the three Gianopoulous siblings. 'But I am of the opinion that your father was responsible for the arms-smuggling. Not Stravros Kalanos.'

'*No!* You are lying.' Christos was on his feet again, spittle flying from his mouth. 'He's paying you to say that, isn't he?' He waved a finger at Lukas. 'This is all a filthy conspiracy.'

The old man sadly shook his head. 'I wasn't privy to the details of your father's dealings, but I have had my suspicions for some time. Suspicions that I should have mentioned to the authorities. That I now intend to share with them. Lukas…' He struggled to his feet. 'It is indeed fortuitous that you are here today, so that I can offer my apologies to you in person.' He beckoned Lukas closer. 'I won't ask for your forgiveness, because I know I don't deserve it, but I want to express my deepest regret for not coming forward before now. For the miscarriage of justice you have suffered and for the ruination of your father's name.'

Lukas stood up, his tall frame rigid with control. The air in the office was suddenly stiflingly hot. Mr

Petrides held out a shaky hand, and for a second Lukas hesitated, before finally reaching to take it in his. Mr Petrides grasped it firmly, patting it with his other hand.

'Thank you, my son. That is more than I deserve. Rest assured I will do the right thing now—'

'Wait a minute,' Yiannis interrupted. 'You are only talking about *suspicions* here, Petrides. You need to think very carefully before making accusations you can't substantiate.'

'No one will believe the old fool, anyway.' Christos snarled.

'It's the truth.' Calista's voice rang out clearly. 'You need to know—both of you. Our father was the guilty party. Not Stavros, and not Lukas.'

'And *you'd* know, would you?'

'Yes, Lukas has told me everything and I believe him.'

'Well, more fool you.' Christos turned on her. 'We all know you've been simpering around your precious Lukas ever since you could walk. He could tell you black was white and you'd believe him.'

'That's enough.' Moving to stand beside Calista, Lukas rested his arm along the back of her chair. 'You need to learn some respect for your sister. Both of you.'

'*Respect?*' Christos sneered. 'D'you really think I'd respect *that*?' He waved a finger at Calista. 'That pathetic ginger creature who has never been anything but a worthless parasite.'

Calista felt Lukas go terrifyingly still.

'What did you just say?'

'Even her own mother didn't want her. Packing her off to Thalassa every summer before she eventually went and killed herself. Calista needs to watch out— that sort of madness is probably in the blood.'

'Christos!' Yiannis tugged at his brother's arm to pull him away.

But Lukas was already there, hauling Christos up by the scruff of the neck, his menacing face only inches from his sweating victim. For a second he held him there. Christos's legs kicked helplessly beneath him, and a look of blind panic came into his eyes as Calista shrieked Lukas's name and Yiannis stepped forward, wildly flapping his hands and tugging at his brother's jacket to try and release him.

'Leave him, Lukas!' Fearing for Christos's very life, Calista tried to get between them. 'He's not worth it.'

Lukas hesitated, letting out a low, savage snarl that curdled Calista's blood. But finally, slowly, he lowered Christos to the ground. Calista could see the effort it took for him to control his fury flaring in his nostrils, throbbing in the veins of his neck.

Hooking his fingers under the knot of Christos's tie, he held him at arm's length, giving him a look of utter disgust. 'Don't you ever, *ever* speak of Calista that way again.'

Christos attempted a grunt.

'Now, apologise.' Releasing his throat, Lukas took hold of his shoulders, roughly turning him to face Calista.

'It's okay. I don't care—'

'It is very much *not* okay!' Lukas's voice roared

around the office. 'This creep is going to apologise, right now.'

'I'm sorry, okay?' Christos looked down at his feet.

'Not good enough. Look your sister in the eye, take back your filthy remarks and apologise properly.'

'I shouldn't have said those things.' Under Lukas's punishing gaze Christos did as he was told. 'I apologise.'

'Sit down.' Throwing him back into his chair, Lukas turned to Yiannis. 'You too.'

Yiannis did as he was told.

'It's time you two learnt a few home truths. Firstly, your father was an immoral, scheming villain who lied his way out of trouble by betraying my father and framing me. Secondly, if I ever hear either of you bad-mouthing Calista again I won't be responsible for my actions. Do I make myself clear?'

The brothers nodded.

'Out of respect for Calista I won't pursue this any further. But that doesn't mean I don't want to.' He fixed Christos with a terrifying glare. 'Because, believe me, taking you outside would give me the greatest pleasure. You don't deserve a sister like Calista. She is brave and strong and honourable and she has more brains than you two idiots put together. Which brings me to my third point.' He paused, shooting a look at Calista. 'You might as well know: I am proud to say that Calista is also the mother of my child.'

Yiannis and Christos gaped in unison, rendered mute by this astonishing revelation.

'Yes, we have a daughter. And one day she will inherit my fortune; carry on my legacy. One day she will preside over the great Kalanos shipping empire. And believe me...' He levelled cold eyes at them. 'This time I intend to make sure that nothing and no one will ever have the power to bring us down.'

CHAPTER EIGHT

'NIGHTCAP?'

Lukas moved over the sideboard and picked up a bottle of brandy.

'Um…yes, why not?'

Calista accepted the glass from him and, taking a sip, felt the comforting burn slide down her throat.

They had returned from an evening meal at a small family-run restaurant, hidden in one of the many cobbled backstreets of this beautiful city. Sitting outside, sharing a table so small that their knees had touched and Lukas had been forced to stretch his long legs out to the side, she had felt blissfully relaxed after the drama of Mr Petrides's office.

The food had been delicious too and, combined with the warm night air, filled with the scent of jasmine and orange blossom, and the indigo sky dotted with stars overhead, she had found herself forgetting her problems for a while and just enjoying Lukas's company. Which was easy when he was being like this: charming, attentive, funny. The old Lukas. Neither of them had even mentioned the hateful scene earlier on—Mr

Petrides's confession and the shocking behaviour of her brothers.

Now, however, Calista suspected that was about to change. Swilling the brandy around in her glass she looked about her, trying to delay the inevitable. 'Your apartment is beautiful.'

'Thank you.' Lukas came and stood by her side. 'Though I could do without the note of surprise.'

'Sorry!' Calista laughed. 'It's just not how I imagined it.'

'Dare I ask how that was?'

'No, probably best not to.'

'Let me guess—all black leather sofas and widescreen televisions?'

'Something like that.'

'And maybe a waterbed with satin sheets? A drawer full of sex toys.'

Calista felt herself flush. Could he read her mind? Or was she just guilty of dreadful stereotyping?

'You mean I've got that wrong too?' She tried to bat back a flippant quip to cover her embarrassment.

'Play your cards right and later on you might find out.'

Calista swallowed. She had walked right into that one.

She moved away from him into the centre of the open-plan room. 'I love all the artwork. Is that an original?' She pointed to a colourful portrait on the wall.

'It is indeed. Modern art is an interest of mine. It's a good investment too. But nothing in my collection really compares to this.' He pressed a switch and the curtains swished to one side and a wall of windows appeared. 'There. What do you think?'

Calista gasped. Before them twinkled the lights of the city of Athens, and in the distance, high above the city, was the Acropolis, glowing proudly against the night sky. 'That's incredible!'

'Even better from out here.' Crossing the room, Lukas took hold of her hand and, opening the glass doors, ushered her out onto the balcony. 'Quite something, isn't it?'

It certainly was. It was magical. Tipping back her head, Calista let the soft night wrap itself around her, drinking in the majesty of the scene. It put life into perspective somehow, thinking about the thousands of years the ancient citadel had been standing there, watching over them, about generations of people gazing up at it, just as she did now, caught up in their own totally absorbing but all too fleeting worlds.

A small movement beside her made her turn. Lukas was studying her, his head on one side, as if she was some sort of fascinating puzzle. Boldly Calista returned his stare, and immediately the flame between them ignited. His dark, raw, intensely primal presence shuddered through her body, making her stomach contract and a heavy beat pulse in her core. Lukas raised his eyebrows fractionally...a small but infinitely telling gesture that weakened her knees.

God, she wanted him so much. She positively ached with it. If he were to kiss her now she knew exactly where it would lead.

But he didn't. Pulling his eyes away from hers, he

gestured to a pair of stylish metal chairs. 'Shall we sit down?'

'Oh, yes—why not?' Desperate to hide her disappointment, Calista quickly did as she was told, all chirpy enthusiasm.

'So...' Lukas turned the dark force of his eyes back on her. 'It would seem that your dear brothers finally know the truth about your father.'

Calista pulled a face. 'They are not my "dear" brothers. I never want to see either of them ever again.'

'Well, that makes two of us.'

He stilled, eyes narrowed, suddenly deadly serious. 'If Christos ever dares to speak about you like that again, I swear I won't be answerable for my actions.'

Calista saw his fists clench.

'I'm still not sure how I stopped myself from killing him there and then.'

'You showed great restraint.' She risked a quick smile.

'I would cheerfully serve a life sentence for that.'

'No, you wouldn't.' Her smile immediately faded. 'He's not worth it.'

Lukas grunted. 'That's true.'

'Thanks for sticking up for me, by the way.' Calista hurried to move the conversation away from the toxic subject of prison sentences.

'That's okay.' His gaze sharpened. 'I meant what I said.'

'Well, thank you. I appreciate it.' Suddenly vulnerable, she looked away, searching for more solid ground. 'What you said about Effie inheriting the shipping business, though… Don't you think that was a bit premature?'

Lukas shrugged. 'No harm in letting them see that the Kalanos dynasty is set to thrive.'

'Hmm…' Calista was far from comfortable with that, but decided not to break the fragile ceasefire by challenging him now.

'I must admit I had always assumed that pair of clowns *knew* the truth about Aristotle,' Lukas continued. 'But judging by the look on their faces today I'm not so sure.'

'I think we were all taken in by our father's lies.' Calista gave him an anxious glance. 'I'm so sorry, Lukas.'

Lukas shook his head wearily. 'Let's call a truce—for tonight at least.'

She nodded. That was fine by her. Given the choice, she would never talk about it again. She would bury the whole wretched business so deep that it would take a nuclear explosion to bring it to light. But it wasn't as simple as that. Lukas had vowed to clear his name and his father's name. Presumably, thanks to Mr Petrides, he was now going to have the evidence to do it.

Aristotle would be exposed for the villain he had been. Which was only right. But that didn't mean the idea didn't fill her with dread. He had still been her father—Effie's grandfather.

Reluctantly she braced herself to ask the dreaded question. 'Can I ask you what you intend to do now?' She placed her glass down on the table between them. 'When will you go public about Aristotle?'

'When I am good and ready. What is it they say? Revenge is a dish best served cold?'

Calista shivered.

'Well, I would be grateful if you could give me some warning before you do...'

'Trying to cover your back, Calista?'

'No!' Indignation saw her temper flare, and she tossed back her head so her hair rippled over her shoulders. 'I'm just saying that if you give me some warning I can prepare myself and make sure Effie is shielded from any press intrusion.'

'Let me assure you that I will have Effie's best interests at heart at all times.'

'Oh, well...thanks...' Her voice tailed off. She had no idea what he meant by that—knew only that the statement held a dark possessiveness that thickened the blood in her veins.

'Speaking of Effie, there is something I have neglected to say to you.'

Now her heart leapt into her throat. If he was going to start talking about applying for custody again she was ready to fight. And fight she would. Tooth and nail and with any other body part she had.

'Yes?' Her green eyes flashed a powerful warning. 'And what's that?'

Lukas deliberately let a second pass. Far from being intimidated by her reaction, he seemed to be rather enjoying it. He picked up his glass and took a sip of brandy, clearly in no hurry to put her out of her misery.

'Just that I realise I have not given you the credit you deserve.'

'Credit for what?' Wrong-footed, Calista frowned back at him.

'For the excellent way you have raised our daughter.'

'Oh.' She finally let out a breath.

'Effie is obviously a happy, well-balanced and frankly exceptional child. You have done a great job.'

'Well, thank you.' Stupidly Calista felt herself flush.

'I can see she is highly intelligent too.' The smile in his voice raised her eyes again. 'Though I suspect she gets that from me.'

'Of course.' Calista played along. 'Along with her humility and modesty.'

Their eyes locked and the tension between them melted away—only to be replaced with something far more dangerous.

'Let's drink to that, then.' Lukas's glittering gaze held hers. 'To Effie, our very special little girl.'

They clinked glasses, and Calista swallowed down the lump in her throat with the swig of brandy. She could feel tears pricking the backs of her eyes, but she had no idea why.

'And to the future, of course.' Missing nothing, Lukas continued to hold her captive. 'Whatever it may hold.'

What, indeed? Trapped by the power of his eyes, Calista had lost the ability to think straight. She needed to get away. *Fast.*

'Well…' She gave an exaggerated stretch. 'It's getting late. I think I'll go to bed.'

She waited for Lukas to say something, to do something. In truth she was waiting for him to stop her.

Instead he remained motionless, those mesmerising eyes still fixed on hers, burning into her, managing to awaken every cell in her body. She watched, tingling with anticipation, as he silently took another sip of brandy, his eyes never moving from her heated face.

'I'll say goodnight, then.' Rising to her feet, she made as if to go, but somehow her feet didn't get the message her brain was trying to transmit and she ended up in a sort of frozen pose, twisted away from him but not moving.

From behind her she heard Lukas laugh—a softly arrogant laugh that had her turning her head, ready to challenge him.

Except that didn't happen. Because suddenly Lukas was there, towering over her. His hands were everywhere—skimming across her shoulderblades, down her back, tracing the curve of her waist, cupping her bottom, pulling her against him. And finally plunging into her hair so that he could hold her steady for his kiss.

And what a kiss.

Hungry, possessive, masterful, it sent a white bolt of craving through Calista, pulsing deep, deep down inside her, throbbing hard and insistent with illicit need. Without a second thought she responded, moulding herself against his body, her mouth greedily crushing his as her lips parted to allow more of this gloriously forbidden pleasure. Her tongue sought his, tasting the hint of brandy on his breath, revelling in the raw, damp heat that mingled between them, tightening her breasts, weighting her core. Rendering her helpless with longing.

'Did you mention bed?'

Sweeping her up in his arms, Lukas moved them both inside, marching through the living area with her clinging to his neck until they were in his bedroom, where he laid her down almost reverentially on his enormous bed.

'Stay like that.'

His throatily sexy command shuddered through her, but the words were superfluous. Calista had no intention of going anywhere. She held her breath as he started to tear off his clothes, undoing a few top buttons of his shirt before giving up and impatiently tugging it over his head, leaving his hair deliciously ruffled. Next came his jeans and boxers and then he was naked before her. Gloriously, proudly naked. His magnificent body gleamed in the dim light of the room…the muscles of his chest were shadowed, hard and unyielding. Calista let her eyes travel south, feeling her mouth go dry as she took in the sculpted V-shape of his pelvis, the line of curling dark hair and then…the mighty swell of his arousal.

But she had no time to feast her eyes. Lukas was on the bed in a flash, kneeing astride her, his hands pushing the straps of her dress over her shoulders, his fingers feverishly working the zipper down her back as she arched up to allow him access. She raised her arms and together they pulled the dress over her head, Calista felt the hard swell of her breasts tugged upwards. Reaching behind her back, she undid her bra, and the hunger in Lukas's stare at the sight of her swollen breasts tightened her nipples to peaks of stone.

They crashed back down onto the bed together again, Lukas straddling her with the length of his body now, their mouths fused with blistering, scorching passion. She moved her hands to grip his jaw, trying to hold him steady so that she could drag in a breath, but he only allowed her one gasp of air before he commandeered her mouth again, continuing his wickedly relentless assault on her senses. Meanwhile his hands had found her panties, pushing them to one side so that he could find her swollen core.

Calista groaned against his mouth, throwing back her head and writhing beneath his touch. *It felt so good. Too good.* It was ridiculous the way he could transport her to the realms of ecstasy just by the touch of his fingers. But she had no defences against this man. This was Lukas—the only man she had ever wanted. The only man she had ever loved.

She was teetering deliciously on the very edge when Lukas stopped, pushing himself back on his heels so that he could pull down her panties and discard them. Calista reached out her arms, desperate to bring him back to her, the small space between them feeling like a yawning chasm. But Lukas had other ideas. Moving her legs apart, he positioned himself between them, shooting Calista a look of dangerously dark promise. Then he lowered his head.

'Lukas…'

She didn't know what she had been going to say and it didn't matter anyway, because as soon as his tongue started to work its magic she was paralysed by the grip of some unknown euphoria. Shooting sensations spread out from her core, fanning through her body, reaching every nerve-ending and pinching them tight. Then tighter still.

'Nice?' Lukas looked up, a wickedly smug expression on his face.

Her only reply was to reach for his head, grasping his hair to push him back down on her again. He couldn't stop *now*.

'I'll take that as a yes.'

His words were muffled against her as he started his glorious assault again. Licking, tasting, nudging just the right spot, over and over again, somehow unerringly altering the pressure to her exact need until he finally quickened the pace and the pressure and she felt herself start to fall. Over and over an edge that wasn't there. To a place that didn't exist.

Moving his position, Lukas gazed down at Calista. She was lying on her back, sated, still reeling from the after-effects. Pride surged through him. *He had done that to her.* She looked so beautiful lying there, her eyes closed, her skin creamy white in the dim half-light of the room. Her hair rippled across the pillow in a tangle of gold. He wanted Calista with a possessiveness that shocked him with its power.

Leaning forward, he kissed her gently on the lips, watching as heavy eyelids slowly opened. Stretching out beside her, he slipped one arm under her body, pulling her on to his chest, catching the look in her eyes as they sparkled, stealing the breath from his lungs with their gloriously erotic promise.

Positioning her so that she was exactly where he wanted her—no, *needed* her—so that he could finally do the thing that seemed more imperative than life itself, Lukas thrust into her, and her ecstatic gasp of pleasure rang like music in his ears. Picking up speed, he felt her match his rhythm, thrust for thrust, taking him—all of him—and giving all of herself in return.

Her obvious confidence filled Lukas with inexplicable pride as she arched her body to take him deeper, her head thrown back so that the wild red curls tumbled down almost to her waist. With a few final delirious strokes they were there, both shattering into pieces, each screaming the other's name.

CHAPTER NINE

As THE ISLAND of Thalassa came into view Calista felt her spirits soar. She couldn't wait to see Effie again. Even though they had only been apart for twenty-four hours she had missed her like mad. But it was more than that. Despite everything, Thalassa still held a special place in her heart.

That place had been well and truly buried the last time she had arrived here—for her father's funeral, less than two weeks ago. Then she had vowed that she would never return, that she would say goodbye to the island for ever. But things had changed. *Everything* had changed.

Lukas had happened.

The previous night had been just incredible. Never in her wildest dreams, her craziest fantasies, had she ever imagined a night like that. The intensity of their lovemaking, the blazing passion between them, had gone way beyond anything she had thought possible. It had been as if all the time they had been apart, all that had happened—the hurt, the anger and the secrets— had been distilled into pure, unadulterated desire. And that had been all it took for them to fall headlong into the madness that had consumed them both.

She had finally woken this morning to see Lukas staring down at her, his ebony eyes deeply serious. Then he had blinked the expression away, leaning forward to touch her lips with a gentle kiss and announcing that they really ought to get up.

But she had seen it—that closed, inscrutable look— and it had been then that it had struck her just how completely she had given herself to Lukas, how recklessly she had laid herself bare. And not just in the physical, earthly sense. By surrendering to such wild abandonment she had exposed her heart and her soul, her most fragile, deeply held emotions. Emotions that she knew Lukas would never share.

And that, she had realised with a stab of sorrow, had been a dangerously foolish thing to do.

They had gone to a small local café for breakfast. Over bowls of yogurt and honey topped with figs and walnuts Lukas had told her he had business to attend to in Athens that would take several days to complete, and had suggested she stay and keep him company. He had left her in no doubt as to what sort of 'company' he meant, and the look he had given her had arrowed straight to her loins, just as he had meant it to do.

With super-human effort she had declined. She had to get back for Effie. She wouldn't have felt comfortable being apart from her for another night, even though her daughter was most probably having the time of her life with Dorcas and Petros. And besides, she had already given far too much of herself to this man.

So Lukas had arranged for one of his charter yachts to take her back to Thalassa—one thing he was never short of was boats. It was crewed by a couple of young Greek gods—or at least that was what they thought they were. Bronzed and athletic, Nico and Tavi leapt about the yacht, winding in ropes and adjusting sails, all with rather more exhibitionism than Calista suspected was strictly necessary. Not that she minded. Even though they were probably about the same age as her, to Calista they seemed like boys. They couldn't hold a candle to Lukas. But that didn't mean she didn't enjoy their attentions. She felt young. She felt sexy. Right now she felt she could do anything.

'Miss Gianopoulous—over there!' Nico called down from his position halfway up a mast. 'Dolphins! And they are coming our way.'

Calista looked to where he was pointing and sure enough there was a large pod of dolphins, swimming towards them. Suddenly they were alongside the boat, all around them, joyfully leaping out of the water and rolling over in the wake behind them. It was such a wonderful sight, and strangely emotional too—as if the dolphins were escorting her home.

Fighting back the tears, Calista told herself to stop being stupid and get a grip. Thalassa was *not* her home. Nor would it ever be. She had to remember that. Last night had been completely wonderful, but in terms of their future nothing had changed between her and Lukas.

What was it he had said? *Let's call a truce—for to-*

night at least. They were telling words. She would be very foolish indeed to ignore them.

Back at Villa Helene, just as Calista suspected, Effie had been having a wonderful time, being thoroughly spoiled by Dorcas and Petros. She was delighted to have her mother back, of course, but after her initial rapturous welcome seemed overly focussed on where Lukas was.

'So when *is* Daddy coming back?'

They were seated outside, at a long wooden table shaded by vines that were trained overhead to provide shade. Dorcas had prepared a delicious late lunch for them all—including Nico and Tavi, who ate with ravenous appetites. There was lots of chatter and laughter, but clearly Effie was missing her father.

'I told you, darling, he'll be back in a few days.'

'How many, *exactly*?' Effie's turned her huge green eyes on her mother, her forkful of food momentarily forgotten.

'I don't know exactly. Maybe a week.'

Effie stuck out her bottom lip.

'Ah, see how she misses her *baba*.' Nico leant across and ruffled Effie's hair, managing to extract a smile from her. 'I tell you what, little one, Tavi and I—we take you out on the boat and show you the dolphins. You like that?'

Effie nodded vigorously.

'That's settled, then. We are here for two more days. We have some fun.'

He shot Calista a cheeky glance which she pointedly

ignored. Now they were on dry land the flirty banter she had enjoyed on the boat seemed misplaced. She certainly didn't want to give these young Adonises the wrong idea. But on the other hand they were only having a bit of harmless fun. What was wrong with spending a bit of time enjoying their company? Why did she always have to be so buttoned up?

Back in England, Calista's friends had despaired of her. Try as they might, they had never been able to prise her out for a night of revelry—seldom even persuaded her to join them for a girly night out. Student nurses knew how to party—that was a given—and Calista was letting the side down by refusing to join in. Sure, she had Effie to consider, but that didn't excuse her total inability to let her hair down at any time.

It also didn't excuse the way she rebuffed the advances of some of the teaching hospital's most attractive and eligible junior doctors. The ones who would have had many a young nurse vying for their bedside manner. But Calista seemed impervious to their charms. She had tried to explain that it was different for her—she had responsibilities. But in truth that was only part of the reason. A very small part. The real reason she had no interest in any other man could be summed up in one name: Lukas Kalanos.

But that didn't mean she couldn't enjoy a few Lukas-free days of relaxation on this beautiful island. She ought to make the most of the fact that his darkly dominating presence wasn't everywhere she looked. That she was being spared the penetrating hooded gaze that seemed to see right through her.

As the euphoria of the night before started wear off, and reality crept in, Calista knew it was time to bring herself down to earth. And keep herself there. So if Nico and Tavi wanted to entertain her and Effie over the next couple of days, why not?

'How many more days now?'

Calista glanced up from her phone, where she'd been looking at nursing jobs on the internet. She would need to start applying soon if she wanted to have a job lined up for September.

'How many days till what, darling?' She didn't really need to ask. She knew perfectly well what her daughter was talking about. She should too—she'd been fielding the same question for well over a week now.

'Till Daddy comes back.' Effie spelled out the question with impatient clarity.

'Um… I'm not sure.'

Calista looked down at her phone again, flipping from email to text. Nothing. That was nine days of silence from Lukas now…and counting… She tossed the phone onto the sofa beside her.

'Still, we're having a nice time here without him, aren't we?' Her voice sounded hollow even to her own ears. And it clearly didn't convince Effie, who wrinkled her small nose in reply.

'I suppose so. But it would be even nicer if Daddy was here.'

Calista drew in a breath. She was trying so hard to put on a brave face for Effie, but underneath she was a churning cauldron of hurt and anger. Two or three days—that was what Lukas had said when she had left him in Athens. Some business he had to attend to. It was unforgivable that he should abandon them like this, with no word of when he planned to return. *He* was the one who had insisted that she and Effie came to Thalassa and now he was ignoring them, leaving their lives suspended until such time as he deigned to honour them with his presence again.

With each day that crawled past, bringing still no word from him, Calista made up her mind that she and Effie should just go—pack up their stuff and return to London. But somehow she couldn't do it. One look at Effie's expectant little face and her resolve crumbled. She longed to see her daddy again. Somehow, in such a short space of time, Lukas had woven his magic spell around her and she adored him. To whisk her away now, with no real reason, would be just plain cruel. She couldn't punish her daughter for her own desperate heartache.

Because that was what it was. Her heart ached as if someone had reached in and crushed it, squeezing and squeezing with an unrelenting grip that would never loosen. And the worst thing was it was all her own fault. Despite denying it, even to herself, she had secretly taken the one night she and Lukas had shared and turned it into something it wasn't—and never would be. The start of a meaningful relationship. And she hated herself, *and* her wretched stupid heart, for being so utterly, blindly foolish.

Because this was *Lukas* they were talking about here. The new Lukas. Cold and calculating and ruthless in the extreme. And how had she gone about protecting herself from this man? By falling into his arms, that was how. By urging him to make love to her, whispering his name against his skin and screaming it out as he brought her to orgasm. By betraying her feelings for him in the most obvious was possible.

Thinking back, she could see how he had manipulated her. The way he had drawn her in, let her come to him, waited like a wolf in his lair as she had come closer and closer. Only pouncing when he had been sure that she was his for the taking. Heat scorched her cheeks at the thought of how she had been used, how wantonly she had given herself to him. And now presumably she was being punished. By maintaining this silence Lukas was exerting his control, showing how little regard he had for her. How neatly she had fallen into his trap.

Well, she could nothing about what had happened that night, but at least she could pull her defences back into place now. And that meant not contacting him—treating his radio silence with the contempt it deserved. On the face of it at least.

She bitterly regretted the one text she had sent him, written on the boat when she'd been coming back to Thalassa, still glowing from the thrill of what they had shared. She had thanked him for a wonderful night. Actually *thanked* him. And there had been kisses. And a smiley face emoji. The thought of which now turned her stomach, even though the message had long since been deleted.

Somehow she had to put her stupidity behind her

and move on. She needed to be strong now—banish all thoughts of a happy-ever-after and behave like the sensible adult she'd used to be. Before Lukas had decimated her heart. She would *not* run away. She would face up to him when he finally returned and do her best to convince him that what had happened between them had meant nothing to her. Clearly it hadn't to him.

'It's time for bed, my love.' Pulling Effie to her, Calista wrapped her arms around her daughter in a tight hug.

'Aw…not yet.' But her protestations were muffled by a big yawn. All the fresh air and sunshine of another day spent on the beach meant that sleep was not far away. 'I hope Daddy comes back tomorrow, then I can show him my shell collection.'

'Yes, well, I'm sure he'd love to see it. But Daddy is very busy, you know. He has a lot of work to do.'

'I know…he told me.' Effie yawned again. 'He's buying lots of big ships. *Really* big ships that cross the oceans full of things for other people.'

Was he? This was news to Calista. She'd had no idea that he was building up the shipping empire again. Not that she was surprised. She could see that restoring the family business—*his* family business, at least—would be a priority for Lukas. And at heart he was an entrepreneur, a highly successful businessman.

'Did he say anything else?' Calista asked the question lightly. She knew she shouldn't be grilling her daughter for information, but curiosity had got the better of her.

'Um…yes.' Effie snuggled into her side and tipped

up her chin to meet her mother's eyes. 'But it's sort of a secret.'

'Oh. Well, in that case perhaps you had better not say.' Calista stroked Effie's hair, deliberately leaving a pause. In common with most four-year-olds, keeping secrets was not one of Effie's strong points. Calista knew she just had to wait.

'If I tell you, you must promise not to tell anyone else.'

'I promise.'

'Well…' Effie struggled to sit up so she could face her mother full-on, excitement shining in her eyes. 'The next big ship that Daddy buys—he's going to call it after *me*!'

'Really?'

'Yes. He's going to call it *Euphemia*. My proper name—not Effie.'

'Well, that is *very* exciting.'

'I know.' Effie felt for a lock of her mother's hair, twisting it around her fingers. 'I expect it must be hard to buy a big ship. That's why he's been away such a long time.'

'Maybe.' Calista pulled her close again for another hug. 'Come on then, you—bedtime.'

She carried Effie through to her bedroom, setting her down and sending her into the bathroom to brush her teeth. While she waited she sat down on the bed and a small cardboard box on Effie's bedside table caught her eye. She had never noticed it before. Picking it up, she lifted the lid and what she saw inside gave her a jolt.

'What's this, Effie?' She raised her voice over the running water and Effie's vigorous toothpaste-spitting.

Effie dutifully appeared in doorway, toothbrush in hand. 'Oh, that. It's a little bit of Daddy's hair.'

Calista stilled, a creeping feeling of unease spreading over her as she looked down at the small lock of hair. 'Why have you got a bit of Daddy's hair?'

'We did a swap. He cut a bit of *his* hair off to give to me, and I cut off a bit of mine to give to him. Daddy helped me because the scissors were sharp.'

Effie returned to the bathroom and replaced her toothbrush in the glass with a clatter.

'Oops!' Calista saw her troubled face reflected in the mirror. 'I've just remembered that was a secret too.'

'That's okay, darling.' Somehow Calista managed to keep her voice steady as Effie re-joined her. But a tremor was starting to ripple through her body, already making her hands shake as the realisation of what Lukas was up to took hold.

'Don't look so worried, Mummy.' Climbing into bed, Effie stopped to give her mother a reassuring kiss on the cheek.

Calista hastily tried to rearrange her frozen features. 'It was only a little bit of hair. I've got lots more.'

'Of course you have.'

Returning the kiss, Calista tucked her daughter up in bed, moved to close the shutters and then silently left the room, pulling the door almost closed behind her.

Walking through to the living room, she seated herself on the sofa and picked up one of the cushions, holding it against her mouth. Only then did she allow herself a muffled scream.

Lukas adjusted the microphone on his headset as he waited for clearance for take-off. He was certainly in no mood to be kept waiting today. As he flicked the switches on the dashboard clearance finally came through and, grasping the controls, he took the helicopter up into the air.

It had proved to be an exhausting couple of weeks. But now he was heading back to Thalassa with his plans for the future finally in place. Plans that would see Calista abiding by his rules. Rules that he would control meticulously, ruthlessly, but above all with his brain—not his traitorous body.

The night that he had spent with her…those hours of wild, uninhibited, mind-blowing sex…now seemed a lifetime ago. As if it had happened to a different man. Which in a way it had. Because Lukas was no longer the deranged lover who had reached repeatedly for Calista's soft body, murmuring her name into the darkness, crying it out on the wave of his release. Actions that had seen him laid dangerously bare.

He had wised up.

Not that he wouldn't still have to be on his guard at all times. Because where Calista was concerned his madness was never far away. Look at the way she had managed to get his granite heart pumping again, firing it with something dangerously close to feeling. *Almost*. And she was addictive, too. He had even asked her to stay on in Athens because he'd wanted more, had been greedy for another night of passion. And then another. But Calista had, of course, declined. Presumably she felt she had done enough already. Enough to bring him to heel.

He had been in a meeting the following day when the worm of doubt about her motives had crept in. Deep in negotiations to buy a multi-million-dollar freighter, he had been enjoying the bargaining, the high-powered cut and thrust. This vessel was another of the fleet that G&K Shipping had owned before their downfall and that Lukas was gradually buying back. And it was going to be named after his daughter. *Euphemia*.

When his phone had beeped with a text from Calista he had scanned it quickly, allowing himself a smile. He would phone later. When he could pass on the good news to Effie that he had her ship.

The deal had been successfully concluded and he'd been shaking hands with the CEO of the rival shipping company when the turn of their conversation had brought him up short.

'So it's true, then?' Georgios Papadakis had given him a quizzical look. 'You're intent on buying back the old fleet?'

Lukas had nodded his assent. He wasn't surprised that Papadakis knew the truth—that the secret was out. At this level the shipping industry was a small and tight-knit group of astute capitalists who made it their business to know everything.

'It is.'

'Well, I admire your tenacity, young man. But buying back the fleet is one thing—finding traders who have any confidence in the Kalanos name will be quite another. That was some scandal you and your father embroiled yourselves in.'

'For your information…' Lukas had fought to control the rage in his voice '…my father and I were entirely innocent of all charges. Aristotle Gianopolous was responsible for the arms-smuggling. Something I will prove to the world very shortly.'

'Is that so?' Lukas had noted that Papadakis didn't look entirely surprised. 'And just how do you intend to do that?'

'I have my ways. New evidence is coming to light all the time.'

That was certainly true. Apart from the old lawyer's testimony, that very morning a new line of enquiry had been opened up. A large South American drugs cartel had recently been busted, and during the police investigations it had come to light that *they* had been the intended recipients of the arms that had been illegally stowed on the G&K freight ship. The last fateful deal that Aristotle had struck.

Lukas was intending to fly to Bolivia that very afternoon to find out as much as he could. He didn't know how long it would take—only that he wouldn't be leaving until he had accomplished his mission. Until he finally had the evidence to expose Aristotle for the man he really was. For all the world to see.

'Interesting…' Papadakis had steepled his fingers. 'And taking up with the Gianopolous girl? Is that somehow part of the plan?'

'I have *not* taken up with Calista Gianopolous!'

'No? Well, that's not what I've heard,' Papadakis had replied. 'I must admit I was surprised. I would have thought she'd be a dangerous bedfellow—especially in view of what you've just told me. Keeping your enemies close. Is that what this is all about, Kalanos? Or is it something else?' The older man's eyes had twinkled mischievously. 'Have you fallen victim to her feminine charms?'

'No!'

'You wouldn't be the first to be taken in by such a siren, that's for sure. And the girl *is* a beauty—I'll give you that. But I would advise you to be careful. Trust any member of the Gianopolous family at your peril. If you are about to expose her father I dare say Calista is keen to save her own skin—and she won't much care how she goes about it.'

'I don't need your warnings, Papadakis.' Lukas's voice had been too loud, carried too much force. 'I've told you—there is nothing between me and Calista.'

'Except the small matter of a child, of course.'

Lukas stilled. So he knew about Effie too.

'Euphemia?' Papadakis indicated the paperwork on the desk between them, which showed the new name that Lukas had registered for his latest purchase. 'It doesn't take a genius to figure out the connection. So the Gianopoulous-Kalanos dynasty is set to rise from the ashes?'

'No.' Lukas's growl had echoed round the room. 'The Gianopoulous family will have no part in this.

This will be a new dynasty, solely bearing the Kalanos name.'

Papadakis had given Lukas a knowing look. 'And yet you have just admitted that the child is Gianopoulous's granddaughter?'

'But she is *my* daughter!' Jumping to his feet, Lukas had glared down at the older man. 'That means she is a Kalanos. That is all you need to know. That is all *anyone* needs to know.'

'If you say so.' Standing up, Papadakis had given him a friendly slap on the back. 'My advice to you would be to make sure you have everything legally tied up. And I mean *everything*. In my experience mixing business with pleasure can be a lethal combination.'

Lukas knew he was right. He had to stake his claim for the Kalanos family. And, although he hadn't fully known it until that moment, stake his claim for Effie as well.

Suddenly Calista's recent behaviour had come into sharp focus. Those subtle little references to Aristotle being Effie's grandfather. About lessening the impact of the truth on Effie. Well, Stavros Kalanos was Effie's grandfather too. Something Calista seemed to have conveniently forgotten. Had she been trying to manipulate him all this time to get him to keep quiet about her father's atrocities? Carry on taking the blame for them himself? Was that what their night together had been all about?

If so, she was going to be sorely disappointed. He might have wanted her in his bed that night—wanted her in his bed every night, come to that—but that was just sex. A basic physical attraction. She might have thought she could wheedle her way into his head, appeal to his better nature, but Lukas had news for her.

He didn't have a better nature. Only a darker, blacker version of himself that had been honed to lethal perfection by his spell in prison.

He had looked back down at the text she had sent him, suddenly filled with rage. All that thanking him for a wonderful night, the kisses, the smiley face emoji. What kind of fool did she take him for? He'd have had more respect for her if she'd begged.

Deleting the message there and then, he had felt in his pocket for the small plastic bag containing a lock of Effie's hair, possessively closing his hand around it. If there had been any doubt before about what he was going to do, if he had felt any guilt, it had been washed away on a tide of cold realisation.

And, should he have needed any *more* convincing of Calista's betrayal, then this morning's distasteful little incident had thoughtfully provided it.

After an arduous ten days in Bolivia, Lukas had returned to Athens earlier today, having successfully secured all the information he needed. Before heading back to Thalassa he had decided to pay a quick, unannounced visit to Blue Sky Charters. He had been about to enter the office when voices from inside had jerked him to a halt.

'You don't stand a chance, man. A babe like Calista Gianopoulous wouldn't look at you twice.'

Lukas's hand had all but fused to the door handle.

'Oh, you think so, do you? I'm telling you—that day on the boat she was definitely giving me the come-on.'

'In your dreams!'

'Don't underestimate the Tavi charm, my friend. It never fails.'

'Yeah, right. If anything it was *me* she fancied. All that "Can you show me how to tie some knots?". I suspect it was more than my rope skills she was interested in.'

'Then perhaps we should settle this with a wager, Nico. First one to get a kiss out of Calista scoops the prize.'

Shaking with fury, Lukas had flung open the office door, crashing it against the wall. Nico and Tavi had scrambled to their feet, and Lukas had waited a beat for the red mist to settle, watching as they'd tried to arrange themselves before him, flushed-faced and sweating. Only then had he delivered his pronouncement—clearly and unequivocally.

'You're fired! Both of you! Get out!'

Now, as he flew the helicopter over the vivid blue Aegean Sea and the island of Thalassa came into view, Lukas could still feel that anger, that all-consuming rage. He could still taste its venom. But it had changed its form, had settled into solid, impenetrable rock that only served to strengthen his resolve.

Calista Gianopoulous had shown her true colours and the scales had fallen from his eyes. Now everything was in place. And she was about to find out the kind of the man he really was.

CHAPTER TEN

AT THE SOUND of the helicopter landing Calista felt her heart lurch. *He was back*. Putting down her book, she leapt to her feet, positioning herself in the middle of the room with her hands on her hips. But as the seconds dragged by and he still hadn't appeared she started to pace up and down, smoothing the fabric of her sundress with shaky hands, her blood pressure rising with every step.

'Kalispera.' Eventually he appeared, throwing her a casual glance before going into the kitchen and returning with a glass of water. 'Where's Effie?' He looked around him.

'She's not here.' Calista ground out her reply.

'I can see that.' Placing his glass down on a low table, he came and stood before her. 'Where is she?'

'It doesn't matter where she is. What's more to the point is where the hell have *you* been?'

'Missed me, have you?' He angled his broad shoulders in a deliberately casual pose. But the look in his eye was anything but casual. It was hard, ruthless, calculating.

'You flatter yourself, Lukas.' Calista averted her gaze from his face and took a couple of steps to the side. He was far too close. 'But it might have been nice if you had told us when you intended to return. Just out of common decency.'

'Common decency has never really been my thing.'

'No.' She met his eyes again, flashing an emerald-green warning. 'I should have realised that.'

He returned an infuriating smile, as if he was enjoying himself, playing with her. 'Well, I can see you are delighted to have me back now.' He looked around him. 'Where did you say Effie was?'

'I didn't.' Calista could feel her colour rising, staining the column of her neck. 'But, since you ask, she is over at Villa Melina. Dorcas is going to give her some tea and then Petros will bring her back.'

'Interesting…' Lukas closed the space between them with a single stride, looking down at her with heated, possessive intent. 'So we are alone.'

'We are. Which is just as well.'

'Even more interesting.' Reaching forward, he took hold of a curl of red hair, twisting it seductively around his finger, his eyes dancing over her face. 'What do you have in mind for us, Calista?'

'I'll tell you what I have in mind.' With a violent toss of her head Calista freed herself. 'Let's start by talking about what you have been doing for the last couple of weeks.'

'What I do with my time is none of your business, *agape*.'

'No? So nothing you have done is any of my business?'

'That's what I said.'

'Then you are a liar, Lukas Kalanos!'

'I beg your pardon?' Lukas's nostrils flared, the chill of his words freezing the air. 'What did you just call me?'

'A liar.' Fear stuttered in Calista's heart but she carried on regardless. She had gone too far to stop now. 'Because that's what you are.'

'I would take that back if I were you, Calista. You are treading on very dangerous ground.'

'No. I won't take it back.' She was riding the wave now, trying to ignore the crash that would inevitably follow.

'Then perhaps I need to put you straight about a few things.' Lukas fixed her with a brutally punishing stare. 'That you of all people should call me a liar is almost beyond belief. You, who have done nothing but deceive me by failing to tell me that I had a daughter for over four years, who would most likely never have told me if I hadn't forced the truth out of you. For you to have the bare-faced nerve to challenge my honesty is staggeringly hypocritical.'

'Not telling you about Effie is completely different. There is no comparison.'

'You lied by omission, Calista. And that is every bit as bad as lying to my face. Worse, in fact. It is even more cowardly. So don't even *think* about trying to defend yourself.'

'I am not interested in defending myself.'

'And, since we are on the subject of liars, why don't we talk about your father? The most heinous liar of all.'

'This is not about me or my father!' she hurled back, hitching her shoulders, wild-eyed with fury. 'This is about *you* sneaking behind my back and taking a sample of Effie's hair to be DNA-tested.'

Lukas remained silent, his eyes narrowing to lethal thick-lashed slits.

'Yes, you see, I know.' Triumphant now, Calista continued. 'So don't bother to deny it.'

'Why would I try and deny it?' Lukas folded his arms across his chest.

'So you admit it, then?'

'It is true that I have had a DNA test done to establish the paternity of my daughter. That's not an admission. It's a statement of fact.'

'A *fact* that you just happened to fail to tell me about?'

He shrugged his indifference.

'Lying by omission.' Calista threw his phrase back at him. 'I believe that was your expression.'

Lukas gave a low growl. 'Taking steps to establish a legal footing for my relationship with my own daughter hardly compares to the atrocities your family have inflicted on mine.'

'*A legal footing?*' Calista spat the words back at him. 'And what exactly does *that* mean? You weren't sure that she was yours—is that it?'

She fired the accusation at him like a missile, but deep down she hoped she was right. Because, insulting though that would be, it was far better than the alternative. The nightmare that had been tormenting her ever since she had discovered he'd taken a sample of Effie's hair.

'On the contrary.' Lukas's voice was as smooth as glass. 'I have never had any doubt that Effie is my daughter.'

Panic made her legs tremble, stealing the breath from her chest. 'So what, then? Why do a DNA test if you already knew the answer?'

A small but deadly smile touched Lukas's lips. 'You're a bright girl, Calista. I'm sure you can work it out. But if you want me to spell it out for you, I will. In order to have any legal control over my daughter I have to be able to prove paternity. Step one is to get my name on her birth certificate.'

Calista felt something shrivel inside her. She could have pointed out that she had hardly been in a position to ask him to sit beside her in the register office and put his name on the birth certificate, but that would only have strengthened his case. And besides, her terrified focus was elsewhere.

'And step two?' She tried to sound rational, but her heart was pounding at a terrifying rate.

'Step two?' Lukas ran a hand over his jaw, as if considering. 'Well, you might as well know. Step two is to apply for full custody of my daughter.'

'No!' The full horror enveloped her like a black shroud. Fists flying, she threw herself at Lukas, pounding at his chest. *'Never!'* The word was twisted into a strangled scream as she thrashed about, lashing out with wild but increasingly futile blows to the solid wall of his chest.

Lukas did absolutely nothing to stop her, taking the assault with a contemptuous calm that only made her more frantic, more desperate. With her hair flying around her face she raised her hand, ready to strike, but with lightning speed Lukas caught it, and along with the other one brought it down so that they were both trapped between them.

'Oh, no, you don't,' he growled. 'You have slapped my face once. You won't be doing that again.'

'Get off me! Let me go!' Calista tried to buck away but that only made Lukas tighten his hold. He looked down at her for a second, before pulling her towards him, releasing her wrists only to wrap his arms around her in a powerful embrace from which there was no escape.

Lowering his head, he whispered in her ear. 'I'll let you go when I am good and ready.'

Calista held herself rigid, her heart raging in her chest, the blood roaring in her ears. And there it was again—that febrile connection pulsing between them, hot and hard and impossible to ignore. *Desire*. Although that was too delicate a name for what she and Lukas felt for each other. It was hunger, craving, infatuation, a greedy obsession that tore at her soul, weakened her, at the same time as giving Lukas all the strength, all the power.

She could feel it now, rampaging through her as Lukas held her tightly against him. Feel the way it sapped her energy, melted her bones to liquid. She let out a breath, giving herself a moment, her body sagging with the sheer exhaustion of trying to fight this physical attraction. This all-consuming madness.

Above her, around her, almost a part of her, Lukas overpowered her—body and soul. Not by his physical strength, although that was undeniably a part of him, but simply by being the man he was. She swallowed against the pain of unshed tears blocking her throat as the reality of the terrible situation hit home.

She loved Lukas.

And right now that felt like the cruellest fate of all.

Loosening his hold, Lukas angled his head so that he could see her face, moving aside the thick twist of hair, the back of his hand brushing her cheek as he did so. Calista closed her eyes. She sensed his head coming closer, felt the soft whisper of his breath on her lips, felt them part slightly, provocatively, inviting his kiss.

With superhuman effort she controlled herself, rearing up and pushing him away. 'You may think you have all the power, Lukas—the wealth and the contacts to gain custody of Effie.' She brushed away the hair that was stuck to her lips. 'But you are wrong. I will never let you take my daughter away from me. *Never.*' Her voice cracked with all the pain inside her, all the sadness and anger, the bitterness and regret. 'I would sooner die than give up my child.'

Taking several steps away, she glared at him, giving him the full force of her temper, fury glittering in her eyes. But inside she had never felt more scared, more vulnerable.

'Aren't we being a little melodramatic?'

Closing the gap, Lukas went to put a hand on her shoulder, but she ducked beneath his arm, turning on her heel and marching from the room. She heard him following her down the corridor as she headed for her bedroom, but she refused to acknowledge the way he propped himself against the doorframe, watching her every move. Tugging open drawers, she dumped the contents on the bed before opening the wardrobe and pulling all the clothes off their hangers. Then, retrieving a suitcase, she unzipped the lid and started to stuff everything inside.

'Can I ask what you think you are doing?'

'Work it out for yourself, Lukas, you're a bright man.' She threw his words back at him before disappearing into the bathroom, collecting up an armful of toiletries and coming back to chuck them into the suitcase. 'I should have thought it was pretty obvious. I'm leaving.'

'Leaving?' Shouldering himself away from the doorframe, Lukas advanced towards her. 'Or running away?'

'Call it what you like.' Pointedly stepping past him, Calista headed for the adjoining room—Effie's bedroom—and began a repeat performance with her belongings. She couldn't stop to think—not now, not with Lukas hovering ever closer, his tall frame right beside her as she stuffed Effie's clothes into her little tiger-shaped suitcase. Glancing at her row of possessions on the windowsill—the collection of seashells, the doll that Dorcas and Petros had given her, the finely modelled sailing boat—a present from her father, which Effie adored—she made a split-second decision and snatched up the doll. The boat could stay there.

'Just in case you should be in any doubt, I am taking Effie with me.'

She had no idea what her plans were other than that she had to get away, right now, whilst her anger still had the capacity to propel her forward. Before real misery rendered her incapable of anything.

'Running away solves nothing, Calista. I would have thought you had learned that by now.'

'On the contrary.'

Brushing past him, she exited the room, pulling the tiger suitcase behind her, swinging the doll from her free hand. Back in her bedroom, she threw it on top of her own suitcase before attempting to zip up the lid. Her chaotic packing meant it refused to close. Opening it again, she saw the doll staring at her with glassy-eyed reproach before Callie turned her over, pressing her down firmly into the muddle of clothes.

'It gets me and Effie away from *you*. And there is nothing more important than that right now.'

'Really? And why do you suppose that is, Calista?'

He was beside her again, leaning over her, barring her way.

'Why are you so desperate to get away from me?'

'Because you are a deceitful, scheming bully—that's why. Because you are plotting to take my daughter away from me. Because—'

Her breathless tirade was silenced by Lukas taking hold of her chin, tipping her face so that she couldn't avoid the inky-black stare of his cruelly beautiful eyes. She felt her skin flare in response, her body straining with tension, but her darting gaze was steady as it was caught in his thrall.

'Because what, Calista? Go on—say it.'

'Because…because I *hate* you!' The words came out in a blind rush of emotion.

Calista took in a deep breath. She had said it before, of course, and it had always felt as if the only person she was punishing was herself. But at least she had come down on the right side of the dangerously thin line that separated the two most extreme of emotions. For she knew she could easily have fallen the other way—knew that as far as Lukas was concerned love and hate were inextricably linked in her neural pathways and always would be. Something he must never find out.

'Hate is a strong word, *agape*.'

Lukas ran a finger over her lips, resting it there as if to silence her. It was only a light pressure but it burned like fire, searing into her until she had to prise open her mouth to free herself from the sensation and take a gasp of air. Immediately Lukas's head lowered, until his mouth hovered over hers, just a hair's breadth away from possessing her with his kiss. A split second away from crashing through her defences…

'Hello!'

At the sound of their daughter's voice Calista sprang away, fleeing the bedroom as fast as her sandaled feet would take her. Lukas was left staring after her, exasperation, raging lust and impotent fury all surging through him in the cacophony of insanity that he had come to accept was part and parcel of his relationship with Calista. If you could call it a relationship.

'Hello, sweetheart.' He could hear her talking to

Effie, her voice unnaturally high, false. 'Have you had a lovely afternoon?'

'Is Daddy here?' Effie cut to the chase. 'The helicopter's outside.'

'Well, yes, he is. But the thing is…'

'*Yassou*, Effie.' Lukas strode into the living room, spreading out his arms in time to catch his daughter as she launched herself at him.

'Yay! You're back.' Throwing her arms around his neck, she snuggled against him as Lukas settled her onto his hip. 'Why were you away so long?'

'I had a lot of work to do.'

'Did you buy my ship?'

'I did.'

'Cool. When can I see it?'

'Well, the thing is, darling—' Calista cut in.

'I'll see if I can arrange a visit very soon.'

'But it won't be that soon.'

Taking control, Calista advanced towards him, reaching out to take Effie from his arms then setting her on her feet and clasping her hand.

'Because there has been a change of plan, Effie. We are going back to England.'

'Aw…' Effie's expressive little face was furrowed with disappointment. 'Why?'

'Because we need to go home.'

'But *why*? I like it here.'

'I'm sure you do. But holidays can't last for ever.'

Effie stuck out her bottom lip. 'Will Daddy be coming with us?'

'No, he won't.'

Big green eyes gazed up at him and Lukas felt something twist inside him. 'Why not?'

'Because Daddy lives here, as you well know.' Calista looked down at her daughter, the patient reasoning in her voice starting to crack. 'Now, I've already packed our suitcases, so if Petros would be kind enough to give us a lift to the harbour...'

'I bet *Daddy* doesn't want us to go—do you, Daddy?'

Two pairs of green eyes swung in his direction, one beseeching, the other glistening with tension and anger and most of all warning.

'You must do as your mother says.' He had been silently watching the exchange between mother and daughter, but now Lukas gave his pronouncement with the full weight of his authority.

He saw the flash of surprise in Calista's eyes before she let out an audible breath.

He had to fight his every instinct, but Lukas knew this was the right thing to do. The clever thing. He had no intention of getting into a slanging match with Calista now—not in front of Effie. If there was any moral high ground to be had he was going to take it. If Calista wanted to pack her bags and leave he wouldn't try and stop her. He could wait—at least a short while longer. And this was just the sort of unreasonable, unpredictable behaviour that would help him in the custody case. A case *he* was going to win.

Yes, very soon he would hold all the cards, and then he would see Calista come crawling back to him. It was an idea that already tightened the muscles of his groin. Once he held all the power he would have Calista just where he wanted her. And that, he knew with blinding certainty, was in his bed.

'Come on, now, little one.' Seeing Effie's bottom lip start to tremble, Lukas picked her up again and held her close. 'There's no need to be sad. I will be seeing you again very soon.'

'Promise?' The word was muffled against his chest.

'I promise. You must go with your mother now, but we'll be together again in no time.'

He put her down, giving her a little pat on the back to send her towards Calista, and their eyes clashed again. Sparks of fear and fight flew at him. She looked like a cornered animal, protecting her young. Which he supposed she was.

He chose to respond with nothing more than the faint quirk of a brow. 'Would you like me to take you back to the mainland in the helicopter?'

The more agitated he felt, the more reasonable he made himself sound. Whether he was trying to convince Calista or himself, or just limit Effie's distress, he wasn't sure. But he did know that the twisting pain in his gut had to be controlled at all costs.

'No, thank you.' Calista's brittle reply snapped between them. 'I am perfectly capable of sorting out my own travel arrangements.'

'As you wish.' But nevertheless he turned to address Petros, who stood in the doorway awaiting instructions, a worried look on his face. 'Petros, please see to it that there is a boat to transport Calista and my daughter back to the mainland.'

'Yes, sir.' Petros nodded solemnly.

'Come on, then, Effie.' With an arm around Effie's shoulder, Calista began to herd her out of the villa. 'Oh, the cases...' She looked behind her.

'Allow me.' Striding back into Calista's bedroom, Lukas picked up the two suitcases and followed them out to Petros's car, where he stowed the cases in the boot. He waited as Calista secured Effie's seatbelt, then leant to give his daughter another hug.

'Don't forget, *paidi mou*, I'll be seeing you again very soon.'

Effie nodded tearfully and, straightening up, Lukas turned to Calista who stood beside him, steadfastly avoiding his eye as she waited to close the car door.

'Calista.' He pronounced her name as a farewell.

'Goodbye, Lukas.' Proud and defiant, Calista returned his valediction.

For a moment they stared at one another, tension radiating between them like a palpable force.

'Until we meet again.' Leaning forward, Lukas spoke quietly against her ear. To a casual observer it might have looked like an affectionate gesture of parting, but it was far from that. The intent in his voice left no room for sentiment or ambiguity. 'I will be in touch very shortly to discuss arrangements.'

'Then you will be wasting your time.' Calista tossed back her head, the rich red curls gleaming in the sunshine. 'There will be no arrangements. Effie is my daughter and she is staying with me.'

Moving past him, she went round to the other side of the car and opened the door.

Lukas was beside her in a flash, barring her way.

'Then you had better get yourself a good lawyer, Calista. You're going to need one.'

Calista glared back at him, eyes ablaze as she waited for him to get out of her way. Lukas watched as she seated herself inside the car, tugging her short dress down over her thighs before reaching across to take hold of Effie's hand.

'Oh, just so you know…' He ducked his head inside for one last parting shot. 'I will shortly be going public about your father. You might want to mention *that* to your lawyer as well.'

And with that he closed the door and banged on the roof as a signal for Petros to leave.

Standing with his hands on his hips, Lukas watched as the car took off, throwing up a cloud of dust as it bumped over the dry single-track road. He was staring at the rear window, at the back of Calista's head, when Effie's little face appeared. With her fingertips pressed to her lips she blew him a series of quick kisses before Calista's arm reached out to turn her to face the front again.

Walking back into the villa, Lukas closed the door behind him and looked around. Strangely enough, he had never felt more alone in his life.

CHAPTER ELEVEN

'PUT IT ON, Mummy.' Effie pointed to the mortarboard resting on Calista's lap.

They were on their way to her graduation ceremony in the grand university hall—something that Effie was looking forward to far more than her. Calista hesitated.

'Go on,' Effie prompted. 'Then everyone can see that this is your special day.'

'Okay!' Giving her daughter a smile, Calista did as she was told and positioned the silly hat on her head, waggling the tassel at her. 'There. Happy now?'

Effie nodded and turned to look out of the taxi window again. Calista stared at her profile. Effie being happy meant more to her than anything else in the world, and it tore at her heart to see how much quieter she had been these past few weeks, how withdrawn. She would have worn a clown outfit to the graduation ceremony if she'd thought it would cheer her up, complete with flappy shoes and red nose. But she knew there was only one thing that would light up Effie's life again, and that was to be reunited with her father.

It had been three weeks since they had returned to

London, and Effie's persistent pestering about when she was going to see her daddy again had eventually settled into a gloomy acceptance that she wasn't. And that had only made Calista feel worse.

But she had fought against it—adopting a relentlessly upbeat and positive attitude, determined that she was going to make up for Lukas's absence. They'd had trips to the zoo and the park, picnics and ice creams. Effie had even been allowed to stay up long past her bedtime, snuggled against her on the sofa. Although in truth this last had been more for her own benefit. Because anything was better than being alone...being left to stare at the whole hideous mess of her life.

Every day she expected it to happen—she would hear on the news that her father's heinous acts had been exposed or a solicitor's letter would come saying that Lukas had filed for custody of Effie. Or both. Every morning she woke with the sick dread of what the day might bring, only to find that it brought nothing. No word from Lukas at all. And, far from finding any sense of relief, all she felt was pain. A tangible, physical pain—as if someone had reached in and ripped out her heart. Because that was what loving Lukas did to her. It tortured her.

The sudden screech of brakes brought her back to the present, followed by the thud of an impact that jerked them both forward against their seat belts.

'What's happened, Mummy?'

'I'm not sure, darling.' Calista looked anxiously at her daughter. 'Are you okay?'

'Yes, I'm fine.' Effie peered out of the taxi window. 'But I think that man is dead.'

Following her gaze, Calista saw a young man sprawled across the road. Quickly she unbuckled her seatbelt. She could deal with this. She was, after all, a qualified nurse.

'I'm sure he's not dead. You stay here, Effie, I'm going to see what I can do to help him.'

Effie nodded obediently and Calista leapt out of the cab to where the casualty lay. He was unconscious, still wearing a crash helmet, and his head was twisted sideways. Blood poured from a serious wound to his leg. A few feet away was the mangled wreck of his motorbike. She knelt down beside him to feel for the pulse in his neck. It was scarily weak.

'I didn't see him!' Beside her the taxi driver was choking with panic. 'He came out of nowhere. I couldn't have avoided him.'

'Call an ambulance!' Calista said firmly. This was not the time for apportioning blame.

A small group of onlookers had started to gather around them—pedestrians and people getting out of their cars as the traffic backed up behind them, horns tooting impatiently already.

'Does anyone here have any first aid experience?' There was an ominous silence.

'You.' She pointed to an intelligent-looking young man on the edge of the crowd. 'Come and help me.'

He obediently stepped forward. 'Are…are you some sort of doctor, miss?'

Standing upright, she realised she must look a bit

odd, dressed in her flowing black and red graduation gown, complete with mortarboard.

'I'm a nurse.' Tossing the mortarboard to one side, she took off the gown and thrust it at the young man. 'Rip this up. We need to make a tourniquet to stop the blood.'

She bent over the casualty again, just in time to see his eyes roll back in his head. *No!* She wouldn't allow him to die. She simply wouldn't.

Grabbing the strip of fabric offered by her helper, she tied it tightly around the casualty's thigh and then, unzipping his leather jacket, started CPR, pumping at his chest with her linked hands as hard as she could, totally focussed on what she had to do.

Minutes passed and still she worked, blotting everything else out, refusing to give up no matter how much her arms ached, how heavily her breath rasped in her throat. She could hear the wail of an ambulance siren in the distance, coming closer. *Hurry up, hurry up.* She could do this. She was going to keep this young man alive.

Lukas held his finger against the buzzer for Calista's flat. Irritation clenched his jaw. She was either ignoring him or she was out. Or, worse still—he felt the irritation turn to something much darker—she and Effie had upped sticks and left.

He should have told them he was coming, of course. That would have been the sensible thing to do. But all sense went out of the window as far as Calista was concerned. Besides, he was looking forward to surprising Effie. And her mother too—but in a very different way.

He had spent the intervening weeks in Athens, working all hours, pushing himself harder and harder to achieve his goals. And he had succeeded, leaving the staff of Kalanos Shipping reeling from the full force of his formidable demands and expectations. As for Blue Sky Charters—the sacking of Nico and Tavi had sent shock waves through that company. The sheer ruthlessness of their boss meant they were now all on high alert to make sure the same thing didn't happen to them.

Aside from business, Lukas had instructed his lawyers to start custody proceedings for his daughter and had collated more than enough information to expose Aristotle Gianopoulous for the monstrous villain that he was.

He should have been feeling pleased with himself, satisfied with all he had accomplished. Instead he just felt knotted up with tension. Far from feeling any sort of triumph, he couldn't shake off the feeling that he had somehow overstepped the boundaries—mistreated Calista right from the start. *Somehow she had made him feel bad.* And that was despite everything he knew, all that she had done. It didn't make any sense.

He missed Effie, of course. Villa Helene felt horribly empty without her there, without her cheery little face opposite him at the breakfast table, without hearing her asking him what they were going to do that day. He had hoped that relocating to his apartment in Athens would improve his frame of mind, but he had found no relief from his gloom there either. Quite the reverse.

Throwing himself into his work had only darkened his mood, made him more irritable, more unreasonable. And the fleeting thought that maybe he should go out, seek some entertainment in one of Athens's many exclusive clubs, had been so repugnant that he'd wondered if he was ill—if there was something physically wrong with him.

But he wasn't ill—at least not in the accepted sense of the word. Deep down he knew all too well where the source of his malaise came from. *Calista Gianopoulous*, that was where. She had crept under his skin, peeled back the protective layers, made him question everything about himself—his motives and his morals. *She had got to him.* His hollow yearning for something undefined had gradually given shape to the certainty that he had to have her in his life. Permanently.

It was a deeply shocking realisation.

And he didn't just mean in his bed at night—although the recollection of what they had done still mercilessly ripped into him. The image of Calista…beautiful Calista…her hair wildly cascading down her back, was seared onto his retina, appearing without his permission whenever he tried to close his eyes. The memory of the way she had looked when he had brought her to orgasm, the way she had felt, tasted, smelled, filled his mind, blocked his sleep and stole his sanity. Try as he might, he simply couldn't get her out of his head.

Which was why last night he had finally given up and made the decision to come to London and sort out this infuriating state of affairs once and for all. How he was going to do it, Lukas no longer had any idea.

But first he had to find her.

The front door opened and Magda appeared.

'I'm looking for Calista. Is she in? Is my daughter here?'

'No. She and Effie have already left.'

'Left?' The word struck fear into his heart and mentally he was already tracking them down, bringing them back, doing whatever it took to return them to where they belonged. With him.

'Yes, for our graduation ceremony.'

Magda held up the gown that Lukas had failed to notice was draped over her arm. Then she pointed over at a taxi idling on the other side of the road.

'That's my taxi, there. Calista went ahead of me because she wanted to—'

'It doesn't matter why.' Rudely interrupting, he ushered Magda towards the waiting taxi and all but bundled her in, following behind her and slamming the door. Leaning forward, he went to speak the taxi driver before realising he had no idea where they were going. 'Wherever *she* says.' He indicated the astonished Magda. 'And make it fast.'

But it wasn't fast. They had been travelling for less than ten minutes when the traffic ground to a halt. There was a queue of vehicles backed up as far as the eye could see.

'There's been an accident, mate.' The taxi driver slid back the glass partition to speak them. 'You might find it quicker to go on foot.'

Hell and damnation. Thrusting some money at him,

Lukas took hold of Magda's hand and pulled her out after him.

'You know the way?' He raised his voice over the sound of the ambulance that was fighting its way through the traffic on the other side of the road.

'I should do.' Magda straightened her skirt. 'I've studied there for three years.'

'Then what are we waiting for? Lead the way.'

'How is he, Dr Lorton?' Calista leapt up as the A&E doctor came towards her.

'Out of danger.' The doctor put an arm around her shoulders. 'You did a great job, Nurse Gianopoulous.'

'And the leg?'

'They've taken him up for surgery now. Mr Dewsnap is pretty certain he can save it.'

'Oh, thank God for that.'

'Seriously, though, Calista, I mean it. You saved that young man's life. Your mummy...' he bent down to speak to Effie, who was busy colouring in some complicated anatomical drawings that someone had found to keep her occupied '...is a proper hero!'

Effie beamed back at him.

'Shame you had to miss your graduation ceremony, though.' Straightening up, Dr Lorton eyed Calista.

'Oh, I'm not bothered about that. At least the gown was put to good use!'

'And this was far more exciting.' Effie joined in the conversation. 'I had a ride in the front of an ambulance and everything.'

'So I heard!'

Calista scooped up her daughter and gave her a big hug. She hoped this incident hadn't been too traumatic for her.

The ambulance that had arrived at the scene had come from the hospital where she'd done her nursing practice and she'd known the paramedics on board. Reluctant to leave her patient, she had accepted their suggestion that she accompany them back to the hospital. There was no way she could have gone on to the ceremony looking as she did anyway—all wild and bloodied. Plus the fact that in all the confusion she'd left her handbag in the taxi, which meant that as well as missing her purse and her phone she didn't have the keys to get into her flat.

She'd called the taxi firm, who had promised to return her bag to the hospital, but in the meanwhile she'd had a shower and found a change of clothes in her locker while various members of staff had fussed over Effie. Judging by the look on her face, Effie had had the time of her life.

'I think I'm going to be a nurse when I grow up.' Wriggling to be put down, Effie went back to her colouring. 'Either that or a shipping *magnet* person.'

'Wow!' Dr Lorton gave Calista an astonished grin.

Calista tried to smile back but her lips had frozen on her face.

'Just like my daddy.'

Lukas's patience was wearing dangerously thin. It felt as if he had been here for hours, seated at the back of this echoing hall of hallowed learning, watching an endless parade of students filing onto the stage to collect their scrolls of achievement, shaking hands, smiling, moving on. What was worse was that there was no sign of Calista. Now he could see Magda, lining up at the bottom of the steps, waiting to be called. This had to be Calista's class. Where the hell *was* she?

'Calista Gianopoulous!'

Suddenly her name echoed around the hall, only to be met with silence, followed by whisperings and some shuffling of papers before they moved on to the next student.

Lukas rose to his feet and moved to the edge of the hall, then made his way towards the front, waiting in the wings. Had Calista found out that he was here? Was that why she had done a disappearing act?

He looked around him, scanning the assembled audience as if half expecting her to have donned some disguise or to be hiding under a seat. Though he had no idea why. Calista never shied away from confrontation. If she were here now she'd be more likely to be laying into him, eyes flashing, breasts heaving, that wild red hair being tossed around her heart-shaped face. Lukas sucked in a breath. God, how he had missed her.

'Magda Jedynak.'

He positioned himself at the bottom of the steps as Magda descended, deftly ushering her to one side as the applause rang out for the next student.

'Where is she, Magda?'

'I don't know!' Moving them into a small chamber off the main hall, Magda looked at him with genuine concern. 'I can't understand it. She and Effie left

well before me…us, I mean. I've tried texting her—
but nothing.'

'Then try again.' He omitted to say that he himself had already left countless unanswered messages
on her phone.

Fumbling beneath her robe, Magda produced her
phone and flicked on the screen. 'One message, but
it's not from Calista.'

Lukas scowled. He had no intention of standing
there watching her read a message from her boyfriend.

'Oh, it *is* Cal—she's using someone else's phone.
There's been an accident…she and Effie are at the hospital.'

'Which hospital?' A wave of black panic washed
over him, consumed him, and his words sounded as if
they'd been spoken by someone else.

'Um… St George's. But she says not to worry. They
are both—'

Before Magda had the chance to finish her sentence
Lukas was gone, his footsteps thundering down the
central aisle between the rows of seats, every head
turning in his direction as he wrenched open the ancient wooden doors and flung himself out into the
street.

'How much longer do we have to stay here?'

'Not long. As soon as the taxi company bring my
bag we can go. Now, come away from the doors.'

Clearly the novelty of being at the hospital had worn
off for Effie, and she was entertaining herself by acti-
vating the automatic doors at Reception. Calista threw

the well-thumbed magazine back down on the table in front of her and yawned. All she wanted to do was to go home.

'He's here!'

Looking up at Effie's yelp of pleasure, Calista saw her jumping up and down, waving madly.

'All right, calm down!' A taxi had pulled up outside, but it hardly merited Effie's ecstatic welcome. She was obviously emotionally overwrought.

'Look, look. It's Daddy! He's *here*!'

Calista felt the world do a giddy spin. *Lukas?* No, he couldn't be! But suddenly there he was, powering through the doors towards them, so commanding, so strikingly handsome that all eyes were on him.

As if watching in slow motion Calista saw him scoop up an overjoyed Effie, quickly casting his eyes over her, and saw the look of grim determination on his face soften as he bent to kiss her on the forehead. Then he turned and straightened up, and suddenly the full force of his attention was on her.

Calista swallowed. Eyes as black as midnight tore into her, immediately shredding the paper-thin patches she had tried to put in place to protect her heart. It was as if he could destroy her with just one look. Tear her apart. This man could control the pumping of her heart, the breath in her chest, the blood in her veins.

He was everything to her, and the more she tried to fight it the more entangled she became. Like a fish caught in a net, the more she thrashed about trying to escape, the worse it was for her.

'Calista.' He was right in front of her now, swallowing her space, with Effie clamped to his side like a limpet. 'What's happened? Are you okay?'

Calista realised that she was standing up, one hand gripping the back of the seat. *No!* she wanted to scream at him. *I am not okay. Every fibre of my being yearns for you...every molecule aches because of you. Loving you has undone me, destroyed me. And I will never, ever recover.*

But none of those words could be said. So, straightening her spine, she pulled in a breath. 'Yes, I'm fine.'

'And Effie?'

'She's fine too. We are both...fine.'

'Then what are you doing here?' Setting Effie down on her feet, he bore down on Calista, placing possessive hands on her shoulders.

'I could ask *you* the same question.'

'For God's sake, Calista.' He frantically searched her face. 'What's going on? Magda said there had been some kind of accident.'

'A man on a motorbike,' Effie helpfully chipped in. 'Mummy saved his life.'

'But neither of you was injured?'

Calista shook her head.

'Thank God!' Lukas's shoulders visibly dropped.

'We were in the taxi that hit him, that's all. Did you say you'd seen Magda?' Calista furrowed her brow, struggling to understand.

'Yes. At the graduation ceremony.'

'You've been to Magda's graduation ceremony?' Her brain seemed to have turned to pulp, like a ball of newspaper left out in the rain. Nothing was making any sense.

'No—well, yes…'

'What were you doing there?'

'I went looking for *you*, of course.'

'Right…' Calista made herself breathe through the fog. There was something about his phrase—*looking for you*—that sent a chill down her stiffened spine. He hadn't come to *see* her, He had come to *find* her. And that had a very different connotation.

She stared into his face, so beautiful but so brutally punishing. A rogue muscle twitched in his cheek and she knew she had read him right.

'Can I ask why?' Her voice held a thread of steel but as she waited the dread of his reply wound around her, tightening its grip. She held her head very still, as if afraid it might part company from the rest of her body.

Silence fell between them. The voices of the people around them were reduced to a soft babble. Lukas shifted his weight from one leg to the other, staring at her with a dark intensity that seemed to be searching her soul.

Or was it his own soul?

For the first time Calista caught the flash of vulnerability in his eyes. Could it be that he was actually battling with himself? Fighting some internal conflict?

His eyes never leaving her face, he took the black leather document case from under his arm and after a moment's pause chucked it onto a nearby seat.

'To do this.'

With a rapid movement he wrapped his arms around her, pressing her against him, one hand moving to the small of her back, where it branded her with its possessive heat.

'And then this.'

Lifting her chin, he took a second to gaze at her startled face before lowering his head and claiming her lips in a blisteringly passionate kiss.

And Calista surrendered to it, melting against him, because there had never been any question of her doing anything else.

She was dimly aware of a ripple of applause, a whistle of appreciation. And then the gleefully shocked voice of her daughter, saying, 'Ew, *yuck*!'

CHAPTER TWELVE

'SHE'S ALREADY SOUND ASLEEP.' Coming through from Effie's bedroom, Calista accepted the glass of champagne that Lukas proffered and sank down onto the sofa. 'She was obviously worn out.'

'I'm not surprised.' Magda came and sat beside her. 'From the sound of it she has had quite a day!'

Calista laughed. Effie had certainly made the most of the day's events, explaining them first to Lukas and then to Magda, and then to the florist who had delivered an enormous bouquet of flowers sent by the patient's family. She had gone into graphic detail over just how her mummy had saved this man's life because he had actually been totally, properly dead, and how she was the biggest hero ever because everybody said so.

'Mmm…yum.' Magda took a sip from her glass. 'Thank you for this, Lukas.' She looked up at him with a mixture of curiosity and blatant admiration.

'My pleasure.'

Calista followed her gaze. Standing with his back to the window, Lukas stood tall and imposing, owning the space even though this was supposed to be *her* domain. She tried to look at him dispassionately— the way Magda would see him. But that only set her heart racing, the way it always did. The way it always would.

Wearing dark grey suit trousers and a fine pin-striped grey and white shirt with the sleeves rolled up, he epitomised the billionaire businessman at ease. Except there was something tense about the set of his shoulders, the angle of his lightly stubbled jaw. His hair had grown since that day she had glimpsed him on the other side of her father's grave—the day that had so dramatically impacted on her life. The severe style he had worn in prison was now softened by loose dark curls at the nape of his neck and starting to fall over his forehead before they were raked back by his impatient hand.

But if his hairstyle was softer it was the only thing about him that was. As she stared at him now, still ex-uding that chillingly austere authority, Calista felt a knife plunge into her soul. Because she knew why he was here. Despite the urbane courteousness, despite the very public kiss they had shared in the hospital, he was here to try and take Effie from her. It was written all over his treacherous face.

'I would like to propose a toast.' His rich, dark voice resonated around the small room.

'Oh, yes—good idea.' Magda sat upright, her glass raised.

'To the two newly qualified nurses. May you both have long and distinguished careers.'

'Thank you. I'll drink to that.' Magda smiled and Lukas stepped forward so that the three of them could clink glasses.

'And, of course, to Calista.'

'Yay! Callie! Our very own hero!'

They clinked glasses again, and Magda leant in to give Calista a big hug. But as Magda pulled away she caught the look on Lukas's face, saw the way his eyes had settled on Calista and she gave a little cough.

'You know what?' She tugged theatrically at the neck of her blouse. 'I think I might make myself scarce.'

'No, don't do that.' Calista reached for her hand, clutching at it in desperation.

'Actually, Magda,' Lukas cut in, 'I want to ask you a favour. Would you mind babysitting this evening, so that I can take Calista out for a meal?'

'Of course.' Magda grinned helpfully. 'Gladly. You go.'

'Oh, no, Magda.' Calista looked at her friend with beseeching eyes. 'I'm sure you must have plans of your own for this evening.'

'No, no plans at all—other than polishing off the rest of that bottle of champagne. You go. And don't hurry back.'

Calista looked daggers at her. Was Magda doing this deliberately? Wasn't she making it perfectly obvious that the thought of being left alone with Lukas filled her with a sickening dread?

'Good, that's settled, then.' Putting his glass down on the table, Lukas picked up his jacket and hooked it over his shoulder with one finger. 'I have a couple of things to do, so I'll pick you up in an hour. Oh...'

He turned, and Calista saw the hard light glittering in his eyes. 'You might want to dress up. After all, this evening is something of a celebration.'

Lukas's dark brows drew together as he watched Calista's mouth close around her forkful of lobster mousse, seeing her swallow, licking her lips with the tip of her tongue to savour the last morsel. They were seated in an exclusive French restaurant in the heart of Mayfair, chosen by Lukas in the hope that the intimate atmosphere would be conducive to conversation. To them starting to sort out their differences. But there had been precious little of that so far.

Polite on the surface, Calista seemed to be paying great attention to her meal. But her body language was stiff, bordering on hostile, as if she was poised, ready to strike back at anything he might say. He, in turn, was still wrestling with the internal struggle that had been plaguing him ever since he had arrived in London, so intent on achieving his aims.

Aims that now floated dead in the water.

The custody case would be dropped. He could never take Effie away from Calista. The idea was preposterous—it always had been. He had been fooling himself from the start. He had been so angry, so hell-bent on making Calista pay for the past, on making up for the years he had lost with his daughter that he had allowed a red mist to cloud his vision, bitterness and vitriol to twist his logic.

Seeing them together in the hospital had forcibly changed his mind. The fact that they were safe, unharmed, had brought such a massive rush of relief it had left him winded, unbalanced. How else could he explain what he'd done—kissing Calista like that, in front of everyone?

No, he could never separate them. Calista and Effie came as a package—a warm, loving, funny, devoted package. He didn't want to tear them apart. He wanted them both. With *him*. Permanently. The question was, just how did he achieve that?

Lukas looked down, fighting to try and order his thoughts. It was hellishly difficult. Seeing Calista again in the flesh, that beautiful porcelain-pale flesh so smooth and warm and incredibly inviting, messed with his head to the point where he thought it might explode. It messed with other parts of his body too.

Suggesting that she dress up this evening had not been such a clever idea. The short gold-coloured cocktail dress shimmered over her curves, catching the light as she turned. With a fitted bust, square neckline and wide shoulder straps it was not particularly revealing—more classy and sexy, a little bit quirky…just like Calista herself. She had swept her hair up into a loose bun at the nape of her neck, the stray curls of hair falling softly around her face giving her a Renaissance, ethereal look.

She looked enchanting, eminently tempting, but most of all *deadly*.

Because Calista was like a drug to him—dangerous and addictive. She made him act in ways that were totally out of character. Firstly his brutish behaviour on the day of her father's funeral—something that he now looked back on with shame—and, even worse than that, the way she was making him feel right now. Raw, hollow, vulnerable. Like no other woman ever had made him feel. Not even close. Hungry with something that wasn't just lust.

Lukas had always known that he craved Calista's body. After all, hadn't he spent years in his prison cell plotting how he would claim her, repeat the sexual experience they had shared, only this time on *his* terms? It had been one of his few pleasures in that echoing temple of misery—something to keep him sane.

Oh, he had dressed it up as revenge, or maybe some sort of sexual infatuation that he needed to get out of his system, but now he knew it was neither of those things. It wasn't just sexual possession he craved—he wanted all of her…body and soul. This wasn't an animal urge. This went deeper—much deeper. To a dark and unknown place where feelings lurked that he didn't want to acknowledge, where emotions that had lain dormant had suddenly started to shift, to rise up, become real. Sentiments that had no part in his life.

The word *love* floated unbidden into his mind, refusing to be batted away. Was it possible that he was in love with Calista? It was an idea so alien, so ridiculous, that he refused to give it countenance. Instead he turned it around to make it more palatable. He wanted Calista to love *him*—that was what it was. The way she said she once had. *That* he could deal with.

He picked up his glass and took a swallow of red wine.

'Well, you have certainly made our daughter proud today.'

'Yes.' Calista allowed herself a small smile. 'But I hope seeing all that drama hasn't been too much for her—you know, gives her nightmares or something.' She glanced at the watch on her wrist. 'I probably shouldn't be too late back.'

'Effie will be just fine.' He spoke firmly, taking control. He wasn't going to let her slip away from him like that. 'First there are things we need to discuss.'

'Very well.' She sat back as the waiter cleared away their plates, folding her arms across her chest. 'Say whatever it is you have to say. But I warn you, Lukas, if it's about taking Effie away from me—'

'It's not.'

His words brought her up short and he saw the look of hope in her eyes as she raised her hand to her mouth in a gesture so charming, so beguiling, that it twisted something inside him. For all her bravado he could see she was afraid of what he might do to her. Once he would have gained satisfaction from that—now it just made him feel like a heel.

'I have decided not to file for custody of Effie.'

'You have?' Relief lit up her eyes and she leant forward to clasp his hand. But almost immediately doubt set in and she let go again, tightly linking her hands in front of her. 'What made you change your mind?'

'I have come up with a better solution.' He concentrated on making his voice even, as flat and smooth as a becalmed sea. 'You and Effie will come and live with me in Greece.'

Calista's shoulders sagged, her eyes clouding over for a moment before her head went back and the fire returned with a vengeance. 'No, Lukas!'

'I think Athens would be the preferred location.'

Lukas continued as if she hadn't spoken. If he stopped to consider her insulting automatic refusal he feared his self-restraint, already tested to the limit, might well shatter completely.

'Though I am prepared to consider other areas, as long as they are not too far from Thalassa.'

'You are not listening to me. Effie and I are going nowhere. We are staying here—in the UK.'

'You may choose the property—more than one, if you so wish, as large and as grand as you like. We will find the very best school for Effie.'

Still he persevered, ignoring the roaring in his ears, his nails digging into his palms as he fought to control the frustration that was surging inside him. The overwhelming urge to sling her over his shoulder and carry her off to his cave there and then.

'I said no.'

'You will want for nothing.' He made one last almighty effort.

A current of electricity crackled between them, waiting to be touched, to do its harm.

'Nothing except my freedom.'

Calista reached for it, whispering the words under her breath.

For a long moment they stared at one another, bitterness and anger holding them both taut, silent. And something else—always that something else that neither of them could control, try as they might.

'I hardly think *you* are in a position to talk about loss of freedom.' The words trickled out insidiously, like a ribbon of poison.

'No. And you are never, *ever* going to let me forget it, are you?' Calista snatched up her napkin, balling it in her fist. 'That's what all this is really about, isn't it, Lukas? You are still trying to make me pay for the sins of my father by threatening to take Effie away from me.'

'Dammit, Calista!' His raised voice turned the heads of other diners and he took a moment, forcing himself to find some control. 'This is nothing to do with your wretched father. This is about Effie being a part of my life. *My life.*' He almost hissed the words at her. 'Not just yours—no matter how much you would like it to be that way. Can't you see? I'm *trying* to find a workable solution!'

'By insisting that we move to Greece?' Still she pushed. 'By putting me and Effie in a golden cage and throwing away the key?'

'Did I *say* it would be like that?'

'No?' She tossed back her head. 'Then tell me what it *would* be like.'

Lukas dragged in a breath, searching for the very last shreds of his patience. 'You would have your own life, your own friends. If you wanted to pursue your nursing career I wouldn't have a problem with that.'

'Oh, how very gracious of you.'

Lukas ground down hard on his jaw. She was really pushing him now.

Reaching forward, he covered her fidgeting hands with his own and fixed her with a merciless stare. 'If I were you, *agapi mou*, I would drop the attitude.'

'Or what?' She fired the shot back at him.

What, indeed? *Or I will make you pay.* The words remained unspoken in his head. Along with the image of how he would do it. With her naked beneath him, on top of him, in front of him. With her screaming his name in ecstasy, begging for more. He could have happily taken her right there and then—swept aside the silver cutlery, the fine china plates and crystal glasses and really given the other diners something to stare at. So strong were his feelings for her. Such was the power she had over him.

He let his eyes close for a second, reining in the crazy madness that was threatening to drag him under.

'Or you may regret it.'

It was a poor substitute for what he wanted to say, what he wanted to do, but as the waiter arrived with their next course he let go of her hands and sat back.

Minutes passed. Lukas began eating his steak. Calista nudged her sea bass with her fork.

'So, how would you see it working?' Her voice was quiet, brittle.

'Working?'

'Well…' She pushed her plate away from her. 'You say that I would have my own friends. Would that be *men* friends?'

Instantly every muscle in Lukas's body tightened, the veins in his neck throbbing with suppressed rage at the very thought.

'No, I thought as much.' Calista gave a hollow laugh of victory. 'Whereas *you*, presumably, would be free to see who you wanted, whenever you wanted. A pretty parade of women on your arm, in your bed.'

'And that would bother you?' He tried to cover his body's betrayal with a deliberately flippant reply.

Calista twitched. 'It wouldn't bother *me*.' She was lying through her pretty white teeth. 'But it would be very damaging for Effie.'

'And if I were to promise that there would be no women?'

'Don't make promises you can't keep, Lukas.'

'Oh, believe me, I don't.' He paused, choosing his words with care. 'If we live together there will be no women in my bed.'

'Yeah, right.'

'Other than you, of course.'

'*Me?*' Pure shock flushed her cheeks.

'Yes—you, Calista. I have every confidence that you will be enough to satisfy my sexual needs.'

'Then your arrogance has taken over your senses.' Green eyes flashed back at him, twists of flame-coloured curls dancing around her heated face. 'Whatever makes you think that I would agree to share your bed?'

'Because I have seen the way you come apart in my arms, felt your nails clawing my back, heard your voice scream my name.' He was going to spare her no mercy. 'You can deny it all you want—do the whole ice maiden routine if it makes you feel better. But you and I both know the truth. You want me every bit as much as I want you. The attraction between us is mutual. And, more than that, it is beyond our control.'

'You flatter yourself. I can control it any time I like.'

'The way you did after your father's funeral? In my apartment in Athens? Even at the hospital today when I kissed you? If that is your definition of control I look forward to being there when you lose it.'

'You know what, Lukas?' Throwing down her napkin, Calista started to get up from the table. 'I'm leaving.'

'No, you are not.'

The booming power of his voice saw Calista glance around her, then sit down again. Picking up his glass, Lukas took a deep swallow of wine, taking a moment to steady himself.

'You can leave when you've heard what I have to say.'

'I've heard enough, thank you.'

'No, you haven't.' He looked down at his wine glass, twisting the stem between his fingers, rotating it once, twice. 'Not so long ago you told me that you once loved me.'

'So?'

'That has led me to a surprising conclusion.' He raised his eyes, deliberately spearing her with their lethal intensity.

Calista stared back at him. Her brow was furrowed

but there was a softness there, a tenderness that clutched at his chest.

'I put it to you, Calista Gianopoulous…' he swallowed firmly '…that you still do.'

CHAPTER THIRTEEN

CALISTA FELT HER face crumple, her cheeks burn with humiliation. Stupid woman that she was. *Stupid, stupid woman.* Instinctively she raised her hands to try and cover her mortified expression, but it was too late. He had seen it. She had caught his complacent look before she had shamefully lowered her eyes to the floor.

He knew.

She might has well have had the words pinned to her back on a piece of paper, the way children did in the school playground. *Calista loves Lukas. Spread it.*

She had spent so long trying to cover it up—from him, from herself, from the whole damned world—that now, when it came to the crunch, when she really should have had her defences shored up, Lukas had brought them crashing down with a simple, elegant theory. But worse than that—far worse…and she could hardly believe her own idiocy here…for one moment of pathetic lunacy she had thought he was going to tell her that *he* loved *her*.

She was obviously losing it. The balance of her mind was clearly disturbed. She was ill.

Reaching down, she felt for her bag. She really was leaving now, and nothing Lukas could say or do would stop her. Scraping back her chair, she pushed herself shakily to her feet and automatically Lukas did the same. She could feel his eyes all over her, spreading goosebumps across her skin as if he had reached out to stop her. But he didn't.

She started to move, weaving her way between the tables and past the *maître d'* at the entrance, convinced that at any moment she would feel Lukas's strong grasp on her arm, bringing her to a halt. But, no. Now she was through the main door and outside, racing up the steps and onto the pavement. She paused for a split second, unsure which way to go, listening to her heart thudding in her chest.

A soft rain was falling, dampening the London streets, picked out by the orange glow of the street-lights. Calista turned right, with no clear idea of where she was going other than that it had to be far away from Lukas. She had embarrassed herself enough for one evening. Now she wanted to hide away and lick her wounds. She walked at a brisk pace, dodging past other pedestrians: laughing groups of young people dressed in their glad rags, foreign tourists putting up their umbrellas, a few late-night shoppers.

Every now and then she glanced over her shoulder to see if Lukas was following her. Her relief was tinged with absurd disappointment when she realised he was not. She strode on through St James's Park, where people were walking their dogs, lovers strolling arm in arm, until she reached the Embankment, where finally she slowed to a stop, leaning against the wall and dragging in a painful breath.

The River Thames flowed lazily before her, lights dancing on the black water, illuminated pleasure boats gliding by, smaller craft going about their business. All totally oblivious to her misery.

Lukas watched her from his position against a tree, twenty or so yards away. She had been easy enough to follow, her red hair bobbing up and down as she had marched through the streets, that golden dress of hers shimmering beneath the streetlights before disappearing again into the shadows.

No matter how dark it was, how much she tried to blend in with the crowd, he could always have picked her out. Even blindfolded, with a hood tied over his head. Because Calista shone like a bright light for him. And like a moth he was drawn to her, hypnotised by her. He was under her spell...

Calista shivered, the fine rain settling on her bare skin, running in rivulets between her breasts. She should hail a taxi and go home.

For the first time it occurred to her that maybe that was where Lukas had gone. Why would he chase through the streets of London after her when he could simply park his elegant self down on her shabby couch and wait for her to return? Or maybe he had done neither of these things but returned to the executive suite of his exclusive hotel to gloat over his victory—the fact that he had won her heart.

'Calista?'

With a gasp of shock she spun around, straight into the solid wall of Lukas's body. Strong arms encircled her, pressing her against him. He felt so good. So right.

'You are soaking wet.' Moving them apart, Lukas shrugged off his jacket and wrapped it around her shoulders, pulling the lapels together under her chin. Then, taking hold of her face, he gazed into her eyes.

'Why are you following me?' She made a weak attempt to confront him, but in truth she was tired of fighting. So very tired.

Lukas gave a short laugh. 'You didn't think I would let you go, did you?' Releasing one hand, he smoothed it over the damp curls of her hair, tucking the stray locks behind her ear. 'I will *never* let you go.' His voice was terrifyingly calm.

Calista stared back at him. Like a deadly promise his words permeated her skin and her bones, squeezing past her internal organs until they found her very core, where they pulsed low and hard and unforgiving.

'And I have no say in the matter?'

'None whatsoever.' He lowered his head, and his breath was a warm caress against her face before his lips brushed hers with a soft, feather-light touch. 'From now on you do as I say.'

'Oh, you think so, do you?' Calista whispered hoarsely.

'Yes, I do.' He pulled back a fraction. 'Firstly I want a proper answer to the question that saw you bolt from the restaurant.' Ebony-black eyes searched her face. '*Do* you love me, Calista?'

Calista waited a beat before finally giving in. 'Yes.'

One hushed word said it all.

'Then say it.' It seemed he was determined to torture her.

'I love you, Lukas.' There was no point in denying it now. She was already stripped bare. 'I wish I didn't, but I do.'

'Hmm… I'm liking the first part of that confession. The second part less so.' He traced his fingertip across her mouth as if to erase it.

'This isn't funny, Lukas.'

'I'm not laughing. In fact when it comes to you and me I have never been more serious about anything in my life.'

'There *is* no "you and me".'

'Oh, but there is.' His eyes shone black. 'I must admit I was afraid that there might never be. I knew I had the power to force you to share custody of Effie, to come and live with me in Greece or the UK or wherever. That didn't really matter. But the one thing I couldn't do was force you to love me.'

'You didn't need to force me.'

'I know that now. And I thank the gods that have intervened on my behalf to make this happen.'

'Lukas…'

'No, hear me out, Calista. There is nothing standing in our way now. We can be a couple—a *real* couple, in every sense of the word. In fact…' He paused, suddenly deadly serious. 'I want us to be man and wife.'

With a gasp Calista freed herself from him arms. 'You're asking me to *marry* you?'

'Is that so shocking?'

'Yes!' She wobbled on her feet as if she had stepped off the highest rung of a ladder. 'Shocking and impossible. It can *never* happen.'

'Why? You have admitted that you love me. We both love Effie. What is there to stop us?'

Calista looked down, unshed tears blocking her throat. 'To make a relationship work…a marriage work…both parties need to love each other.' Her voice was very small. 'Not just one.'

Lukas let his eyes travel slowly over her dejected but still defiant figure. Her head was bent, her torso swamped by the jacket that hung over her shoulders. Raindrops sparkled in her hair and as he reached for her, bringing her close and tipping her head, he could see the glitter of tears in her eyes.

And the shackles of his pride fell away.

Suddenly, miraculously, he was able to say what he thought—accept what he had always known. He was free to face up to the truth and express the one thing that mattered—the only thing that mattered. He was in love with Calista. He had never said it before, even to himself, but it was a simple incontrovertible fact.

He sounded out the words in his head. *I love you, Calista.* They seemed surprisingly natural—as if they had always been there waiting to be spoken. But there was also a strange sense of loss. Because by giving his heart to Calista he was losing a part of himself. The bitter and resentful part…the hostile, vengeful part. It had been with him so long, knew him so well, that he had thought it made up the man he was.

But now he knew differently. Without even trying,

without even knowing it, Calista had slain that vicious monster and set him free. Free to love her.

And yet she had no idea what she had done.

Taking her face in his hands, he turned it towards him and caught the pain in her eyes, the hurt. He wanted to take it away with a blistering kiss. He longed to show his love for her, right there and then, and not by using mere words. But that would have to come later. Right now words would have to do. If only he could find them.

'If love is the issue then there is no impediment to our marriage.'

Calista stared back at him, uncomprehending. Which wasn't surprising, considering he'd sounded like a jumped-up lawyer or a jerk—or both.

'What I'm trying to say is…' He rubbed the pads of his thumbs along her jaw. 'What I'm trying to tell you…'

'Yes?'

Oh, for God's sake, man.

'Calista.' He pulled in a breath. 'You are the most obstinate, infuriating, maddeningly wonderful woman that I have ever had the good fortune to come across.' Calista blinked back at him. 'And I love you with all my heart.'

There was a stunned silence.

'No.' Calista pulled away. 'You can't.'

'Yes, Calista, I do.'

'You're just saying that.' She cast about as if looking for an answer, her eyes following the inky-black river. 'This is just some plan you have come up with to try and trick me. Or you think it's what I want to hear. Or maybe it's some sort of aberration.'

'You mean I would have to be suffering some sort of mental illness to be in love with you?' The corner of his mouth quirked.

'Yes—no. I don't know.' Looking back at him, she frowned solemnly. 'Maybe...'

'Then I am indeed afflicted.'

He smiled at her now...an open, guileless smile that was rewarded with a small twitch of her lips. But that wasn't enough—he wanted much more. So he waited, his head on one side, his eyebrows raised, his eyes holding hers. And finally he was rewarded with a real smile, so dazzling, so heartfelt that it threatened to undo him completely.

He pulled her back into his arms, burying his face in her wet hair, inhaling her uniquely wonderful scent mixed with the dampness of a London night.

'I love you, Calista. Whether you believe it or not. Whether you want me to or not. If that makes me crazy in the head...' he pulled back to look into her face again '... Then I'm guilty as charged.'

'Oh, Lukas!'

'And I want to marry you more than anything in the world.' Dropping down onto one knee, Lukas took hold of her hands and clasped them to his chest. 'Calista Gianopoulous, would you do me the greatest honour of becoming my wife?'

Calista looked down at him, her eyes shining with love and tears and with what Lukas desperately hoped was the most important 'yes' of his life. From somewhere behind them Big Ben began pealing the hour.

He counted three, four, five agonising chimes before Calista finally spoke.

'Yes, Lukas Kalanos.' Her voice cracked and tears started to run down her cheeks. Hysteria was not far away. 'My answer is yes. I *will* marry you!'

Relief and elation and pure, fathomless love sprang Lukas to his feet and he held out his arms for Calista to fall into, wrapping her in a crushing embrace.

Big Ben's final toll rang out unheard. Because as their eyes closed and their lips met for this most precious, tender kiss time for Calista and Lukas stood perfectly still.

'Does this look okay?' Calista stood before Lukas wearing one of his pristine shirts over the gold cocktail dress, artfully tied around her waist, sleeves rolled up. 'I don't want to go back looking like a dirty stop-out.'

'But that's exactly what you are, *agape*.' Lukas pulled her towards him, linking his arms around her waist. 'And a very sexy one at that.'

Pressed so closely against him, Calista felt the stirrings of his arousal.

'How about we ring Magda and say we will be another hour or so?'

'No!' With a laugh she pushed him away.

Having spent the night at Lukas's hotel, they had only just managed to get themselves up and showered and dressed—all of those things repeatedly interrupted by more carnal matters. And this after a night of such passion, such intense emotional and physical joy, that it didn't seem possible that they could still crave more of one another. But of course they did. And always would.

'We can't impose on Magda any more.' She gave him a quick kiss. 'And, besides, Effie will be waiting for us. I can't wait to tell her we're getting married!'

'You think she will be pleased?'

'Pleased? She'll be *ecstatic*! She adores you, Lukas, surely you know that? Just like her mother does.' Her eyes shone with love. 'Plus, of course, she'll get to be bridesmaid.'

'Whatever did I do to deserve you two?' Suddenly serious, Lukas pulled back to look into her eyes. 'I've been such a fool, Calista—such an idiot, trying to control you rather than letting myself love you, mistaking the intensity of my feelings for anger and revenge when all the time I was just madly in love with you.'

'You had every right to be filled with fury after what my father did to you. What *I* did.'

'No, not you, Calista. You were completely blameless. I concocted that story because I couldn't believe you'd come to me that night simply because you wanted me.'

'Not just wanted you, Lukas—*loved* you. Even then. But I couldn't tell you. I let my pride get in the way of admitting the truth.'

'I love your pride. And your smile and your scowl and your temper and your big heart. Especially your big heart.' He gave her a lopsided smile. 'Even when it means I end up having to reinstate members of my own staff.'

Calista grinned. 'Thanks for agreeing to do that. I'm

sure Nico and Tavi have learnt their lesson, and you said yourself they're good workers. It was just a bit of silly chest-beating, you know that.'

'I do now.'

For a second they gazed at one another in silence. Then Calista bit down on her lip.

'Come on—spill.' Lukas searched her face. 'What's troubling you now?'

'I was just thinking about my father.'

'Ah.' The hollow sound rang with bitterness. 'I'd rather not think about him.'

'But we have to.' Calista felt the familiar feeling of torture start to seep into her happiness. 'I'm assuming you still intend to expose what he did?'

Lukas shook his head and, reaching for her hands, held them against his chest. 'No, not now. Not knowing how it would impact on you.'

He moved over to the table and pulled a sheaf of papers from the document case Calista remembered he had been holding when he had arrived at the hospital.

'Here. These are for you.'

'What are they?' Nervously she reached to take them from his outstretched hand.

'Evidence of Aristotle's involvement in the armssmuggling. How he wrongly implicated my father and me. It's all in there.'

'Oh, God…' Calista's free hand flew to cover her mouth. 'I'm so sorry, Lukas.'

'No more apologies, Calista. Please. Let's put the past behind us. I don't care about any of it any more. You can chuck it on the fire, shred it—do whatever you want with it. The future is all that matters now. You, me and Effie. The most wonderful future I could ever wish for.'

Calista looked down at the hateful papers in her hand. There was nothing she would like to do more than destroy them. But she knew with depressing certainty that she couldn't. Destroying evidence didn't destroy the past. Her father's evil deeds couldn't be eradicated. And the damage he had inflicted along the way to Stavros and to Lukas...

No, she couldn't keep the burden of that secret. She wouldn't be able to live with herself.

'I'm going to take these to the police.' She held up the papers with a shaky hand.

Lukas stared at her in alarm. 'No, Calista, you don't have to.'

'Yes—yes, I do.'

'Please think very carefully before you do anything rash. The fall-out could be pretty nasty.'

'I know that. But you and your father have taken the blame for Aristotle's crimes for far too long. It's time the truth came out.'

'And you're sure about this?'

'Yes, quite sure. My loyalties are to *you* now—you and Stavros, the Kalanos family. Very soon I will bear the Kalanos name, and Effie too, once the paperwork is sorted. I will no longer be a Gianopoulous and neither will she. Maybe when the truth is out I will be able to move on, put my traitorous bloodline behind me. Free myself of the ties of my father.'

'Calista Kalanos. I can't tell you how good that sounds.'

'Mmm…for me too.'

They kissed again.

'You are extraordinarily brave, Calista—you know that, don't you?'

'Not brave. Just doing what has to be done.'

'Then I will be right there beside you to support you. No one will lay any blame at *your* door. I will make sure of that. If they try they will have me to answer to.'

'You and me against the world, eh?'

'No, not against it. Owning it—making it ours. You and Effie are my world. All I could ever want and all I could ever ask for. Except maybe…'

'Yes, go on—what?'

'Maybe a little brother or sister for Effie. Or both. Or a couple of each… In fact maybe we should start now.'

Laughing, Calista pushed herself back from his embrace to gaze into his midnight eyes. 'I love you, Lukas. So, *so* much.'

'I love you too, Calista, more than words can say. And I can't wait to spend the rest of my life with you.'

'Me too, Lukas,' Calista whispered softly against his lips. 'Me too.'

* * * * *

If you enjoyed
THE GREEK'S PLEASURABLE REVENGE
why not read these other
SECRET HEIRS OF BILLIONAIRES *stories?*

THE SECRET TO MARRYING MARCHESI
by Amanda Cinelli
DEMETRIOUS DEMANDS HIS CHILD
by Kate Hewitt
THE DESERT KING'S SECRET HEIR
by Annie West
THE SHEIKH'S SECRET SON
by Maggie Cox
THE INNOCENT'S SHAMEFUL SECRET
by Sara Craven

Available now!

Available June 20, 2017

#3537 THE PREGNANT KAVAKOS BRIDE
One Night With Consequences
by Sharon Kendrick

Ariston Kavakos makes impoverished Keeley Turner a proposition: a month's employment on his island, at his command. Soon her resistance to their sizzling chemistry weakens! But when there's a consequence, Ariston makes one thing clear: Keeley *will* become his bride...

#3538 A RING TO SECURE HIS CROWN
by Kim Lawrence

Why is Sabrina Summerville so drawn to her betrothed's dangerous younger brother, Prince Sebastian? An abdication makes Sebastian ruler—so he must marry Sabrina himself! If the sparks between them are any indication, their marriage is going to be explosive...

#3539 SICILIAN'S BABY OF SHAME
Billionaires & One-Night Heirs
by Carol Marinelli

When chambermaid Sophie encounters Bastiano Conti, his raw sexuality tempts her untouched body! Bastiano's conscience flickers when he discovers that after their unforgettable indiscretion, Sophie was left destitute and pregnant. He must claim his child...by seducing Sophie into wearing his ring!

#3540 SALAZAR'S ONE-NIGHT HEIR
The Secret Billionaires
by Jennifer Hayward

Alejandro Salazar takes the opportunity to expose the Hargrove family—by working in their stables! Alejandro mustn't be distracted by Hargrove heiress Cecily's innocent passion. But when their bliss results in pregnancy Alejandro will restore his family's honor... with a diamond ring!

HPCNM0617RA

#3541 THE SECRET KEPT FROM THE GREEK
Secret Heirs of Billionaires
by Susan Stephens
Damon Gavros and Lizzie Montgomery's searing desire sweeps her back to their exquisite night eleven years ago! But Lizzie's hiding something, and Damon's determination to discover it is relentless. Until he finds out Lizzie's secret is his daughter!

#3542 THE BILLIONAIRE'S SECRET PRINCESS
Scandalous Royal Brides
by Caitlin Crews
Princess Valentina swaps places with her identical twin, but she quickly realizes that fooling her "boss" Achilles Casilieris is going to be difficult when he makes her burn with longing. Their powerful attraction will push Valentina's façade to the limit...

#3543 WEDDING NIGHT WITH HER ENEMY
Wedlocked!
by Melanie Milburne
Allegra Kallas both *detests* and longs for Draco Papandreou, so she's horrified when he's the only man who can save her family's business. Draco has a sinful plan: he'll make Allegra his wife and seduce her into his bed...

#3544 CLAIMING HIS CONVENIENT FIANCÉE
by Natalie Anderson
When Catriona breaks into her old family mansion to retrieve an heirloom, she doesn't expect to get caught by Alejandro Martinez! Kitty's recklessness ignites Alejandro's animal urges. So when Kitty is mistaken for his fiancée, he'll take full advantage—and unleash their hunger!

YOU CAN FIND MORE INFORMATION ON UPCOMING HARLEQUIN® TITLES, FREE EXCERPTS AND MORE AT WWW.HARLEQUIN.COM.

HPCNM0617RB

*Ariston Kavakos makes impoverished Keeley Turner a
proposition: a month's employment on his island, at his
command. Soon her resistance to their sizzling chemistry
weakens! But when there's a consequence, Ariston makes
one thing clear: Keeley* will *become his bride…*

Read on for a sneak preview of
Sharon Kendrick's book
THE PREGNANT KAVAKOS BRIDE

ONE NIGHT WITH CONSEQUENCES
Conveniently wedded, passionately bedded!

"You're offering to buy my baby? Are you out of your
mind?"

"I'm giving you the opportunity to make a fresh start."

"Without my baby?"

"A baby will tie you down. I can give this child everything
it needs," Ariston said, deliberately allowing his gaze to drift
around the dingy little room. "You cannot."

"Oh, but that's where you're wrong, Ariston," Keeley
said, her hands clenching. "You might have all the houses
and yachts and servants in the world, but you have a great
big hole where your heart should be—and therefore you're
incapable of giving this child the thing it needs more than
anything else!"

"Which is?"

"Love!"

Ariston felt his body stiffen. He loved his brother
and once he'd loved his mother, but he was aware of his
limitations. No, he didn't do the big showy emotion he

suspected she was talking about, and why should he, when he knew the brutal heartache it could cause? Yet something told him that trying to defend his own position was pointless. She would fight for this child, he realized. She would fight with all the strength she possessed, and that was going to complicate things. Did she imagine he was going to accept what she'd just told him and play no part in it? Politely dole out payments and have sporadic weekend meetings with his own flesh and blood? Or worse, no meetings at all? He met the green blaze of her eyes.

"So you won't give this baby up and neither will I," he said softly. "Which means that the only solution is for me to marry you."

He saw the shock and horror on her face.

"But I don't want to marry you! It wouldn't work, Ariston—on so many levels. You must realize that. Me, as the wife of an autocratic control freak who doesn't even like me? I don't think so."

"It wasn't a question," he said silkily. "It was a statement. It's not a case of if you will marry me, Keeley—just when."

"You're mad," she breathed.

He shook his head. "Just determined to get what is rightfully mine. So why not consider what I've said, and sleep on it and I'll return tomorrow at noon for your answer—when you've calmed down. But I'm warning you now, Keeley—that if you are willful enough to try to refuse me, or if you make some foolish attempt to run away and escape—" he paused and looked straight into her eyes "—I will find you and drag you through every court in the land to get what is rightfully mine."

Don't miss
THE PREGNANT KAVAKOS BRIDE
available July 2017 wherever
Harlequin Presents® books and ebooks are sold.

www.Harlequin.com

HARLEQUIN
Presents

Next month, look out for the final installment of the thrilling The Secret Billionaires trilogy! Three extraordinary men accept the challenge of leaving their billionaire lifestyles behind. But in *Salazar's One-Night Heir* by Jennifer Hayward, Alejandro must also seek revenge for a decades-old injustice...

Tycoon Alejandro Salazar will take any opportunity to expose the Hargrove family's crime against his—including accepting a challenge to pose as their stable groom! His goal in sight, Alejandro cannot allow himself to be distracted by the gorgeous Hargrove heiress...

Her family must pay, yet Alejandro can't resist innocent Cecily's fiery passion. And when their one night of bliss results in an unexpected pregnancy Alejandro will legitimize his heir and restore his family's honor...by binding Cecily to him with a diamond ring!

The Secret Billionaires

Challenged to go undercover—but tempted to blow it all!

Di Marcello's Secret Son
by Rachael Thomas

Xenakis's Convenient Bride
by Dani Collins
Available now!

Salazar's One-Night Heir
by Jennifer Hayward
Available July 2017!

Stay Connected:
www.Harlequin.com

f /HarlequinBooks

t @HarlequinBooks

p /HarlequinBooks

HP06080